Poetic Licence

Antonio Di Angelo

ISBN 978-0-9566310-0-8

Published by Antonio Di Angelo

Disclaimer

This book is a work of fiction. Names, characters, places and incidents are either products of the author's imagination or are used fictitiously. Any resemblance to actual events, places or people (living or dead) is coincidental. This book may use trademarks in the context of fair comment. Such use does not constitute an endorsement or authorisation of this work by the trademark owner.

CONTENTS

PART ONE

PART TWO

PART ONE

Vicky the Vampire Goddess – The Beginning

Deep in the depths of a medieval Pembrokeshire castle was a twenty one year old undergraduate anthropology student at Cambridge University. Vicky loved exploring castles, archaeological and historic sites, little did she realise that she was on a university field trip that would change her life forever. She was destined to be at the centre of a struggle for survival between vampires and humans and her life would never be the same again.

It was mid-afternoon in the scorching September heat. Emily dragged fellow anthropological student Vicky by the arm and led her into an adjacent room away from their classmates. "Where are we going?" asked Vicky "our group is in the other room; we're going to get lost Emily!" Emily put her fingers on Vicky's lips to quieten her "shhh, my love, let's explore together, it's so much more fun." Vicky always hated it when Emily called her 'love'; she knew Emily was attracted to her and it made her feel queasy. "No Emily, we mustn't" Vicky insisted, pushing her away and trying to release herself from Emily's tight grip of her right wrist. Emily knew Vicky would win any physical battle, Vicky was 5'8" and very athletic whereas she was 5'4", svelte and abhorred any form of sports or physical activity.

Emily released her grip of Vicky's right wrist, "okay, how about we explore for five minutes, c'mon you know how much I want to do this?" Vicky rolled her eyes and nodded "okay, five minutes only, it's now 3.20pm." Emily grabbed Vicky's hand and they went into the nearest chamber room, it was full of bookcases, vases and what looked like medical measuring equipment. As Emily walked to one edge of the room she noticed the sun shining on a knight's helmet, she turned to Vicky and exclaimed "ain't this cool" pointing with her right hand to the knight.

Vicky meanwhile was lost in the alcove housing the medical measuring equipment, "what you doing over there?" Emily beckoned. When Vicky didn't answer she went over and saw Vicky kneeling on the ground with her head in a cabinet. "What are you doing V?" she asked, Vicky didn't respond but continued to move deeper into the cabinet, "Vicky, what is in there?" Emily asked worriedly. "Shhh my love" Vicky said softly, "these are ancient artefacts; it looks like some kind of prescription or recipe."

Emily frowned and crossed her arms to express her annoyance at Vicky's fascination with her new found artefacts. Whenever Vicky's curiosity was piqued she would continue investigating until her curiosity was satiated. "This stuff is so cool, I'm gonna borrow it" Vicky said, "what?" Emily gasped "you can't do that, they're gonna know about it." "No they won't" Vicky said as she grinned cheekily. Emily raised her eyebrows and looked bemused as Vicky pulled out a scroll, an oblong silver container and a golden trinket from the cabinet and put it carefully into her backpack before pushing the cabinet door shut.

There was a metallic plate in the shape of a palm embossed with gold next to the door handle. "See" Vicky said, pointing to the palm "try and open it, use your right hand," she got up and moved away from the cabinet to let Emily kneel down. Emily pressed her right hand against the metallic plate "it's quite cold" Emily complained, "yeah I know, now pull the handle" Vicky responded. Emily pulled the handle with her left hand but it didn't budge. "Look I'll show you" Vicky said as she knelt down next to Emily and put her right hand on the metallic plate. She pulled the handle with her left hand and the cabinet door opened easily.

"Oh my god, how the hell did you do that V, are you some freak?" Emily asked inquisitively. Vicky closed the door, got up and grabbed Emily by both hands "let's get out of here but I want you to promise me you won't tell anyone about the cabinet?" Emily replied reluctantly "promise." They both headed back towards where they had left their classmates. As they rejoined their classmates, Vicky tried desperately to conceal her excitement. All she wanted to do was return to her halls of residence and investigate the artefacts in her backpack. The students went to the courtyard for a final talk by the castle's curator before boarding their coach home.

Vicky didn't want to examine the artefacts in front of Emily so when they arrived back at the halls of residence she feigned illness and told Emily she was going to rest.

As soon as Vicky got to her room, she locked her door, drew her curtains and put on the lights. She threw the contents of her backpack onto her bed and earnestly examined the artefacts. The scrolls intrigued her the most, she remembered seeing writing at one edge of the scroll glittering in the afternoon sun but the ink was matt black so she knew it could not be theoretically possible. As she unrolled the scroll she felt a sudden pain in her spine and her vision became slightly blurred.

She rubbed her eyes and looked at the scroll again, in the centre was an image in pencil of a girl who looked exactly like her. She immediately threw the scroll on the floor. After a few minutes when she had regained her composure, she knelt down on her bedroom floor and picked up the scroll. She looked closely at the figure; it seemed to be a mirror image of her. The figure had hair the same length as her and had hair combed in the same direction. She felt a chill flow through her body.

There was some writing at the bottom of the figure, she looked closely and saw that the letters were written very strangely, as if forming some form of equation, it seemed to spell the word 'Nyxz'. This was too freaky to be real so she rolled up the scroll, bundled it together with the silver container and golden trinket and put it into a carrier bag before hiding it at the back of her wardrobe.

Vicky needed some fresh air as her room suddenly felt too claustrophobic. She ran down the corridor and used the back stairwell to exit her block to avoid bumping into any of her friends. After sitting in the garden outside her dorm block for ten minutes, she became uneasy, she felt someone was watching her. She stared up at her dorm block, there didn't seem to be anything unusual going on and she couldn't see anyone looking at her. She got up and dusted the grass off from her jeans. Before heading back to her room Vicky stopped off at the I.T. suite. There were a few students using the suite but thankfully she didn't recognise any of them.

She sat down at the desktop computer near the window and began researching the history of Pembrokeshire castle and the ancient scrolls. There were many search results but none of them mentioned anything about the scrolls. There was a blog post on futureology.com indicating that during the Middle Ages a war between vampires and humans took place, and that Pembroke castle was the last outpost of the Vampires, it seemed the vampires were all but destroyed. Vicky enjoyed the whole vampire saga, she enjoyed reading Twilight, True Blood and watching re-runs of Buffy on DVD.

She typed 'Nyxz' into the search engine and found many results which indicated that Nyxz was a surname or a name of a company. After scrolling down to page twenty, a link to Furtureology.com came up, the post by 'The Count' stated that Nyxz was the Vampire goddess. The post said that the goddess would emerge at a time when the vampire race was in danger of being destroyed; she would be the one who unites all vampires and ensures that the vampires would survive the coming persecution. She would be human, to ensure she would evade detection but as the war grew, she would transform into a vampire. She would never be an ordinary vampire for her blood would hold the key to the vampires' survival. The post left Vicky intrigued.

Vicky knew that scientists had developed a new DNA serum test that could easily identify vampires and that vampire pogroms were fairly common. She figured that the blood of the vampire goddess would play a role in beating the DNA serum test.

She sat back in her chair and looked out of the window into the dark night sky. She wondered for a moment if the artefacts and the forum post had anything to do with her. In all her life she had never met a vampire, the closest she came to being a vampire was at a teenage fancy dress party when she dressed up as a sexy vamp. But she had an eerie feeling that something was about to change, as she looked up again into the starry night she sensed that her life would never be the same again.

Her phone suddenly bleeped causing her to jump in her chair; she was still spooked and on edge after everything that had just happened. She checked her phone, it was a text message from Emily asking her where she was. Emily had knocked at her dorm door and got no answer so was relaxing with Brenda and Alessia in the cafeteria. Vicky looked around, everything in the I.T. suite was normal. The other students were busy engrossed listening to music with headphones on or tapping away on instant messaging chat services. She breathed a welcome sigh of relief; maybe she just had an overactive imagination.

Before going back to her room, Vicky headed to the dorm cafeteria, Emily was busy chatting away with Brenda and Alessia and they all were looking at Alessia's laptop. As she approached the trio, Emily shouted "V, check this out, Cory Hunter is now dating Jessica May, y'know, that super talented violinist". "Really, isn't he like 42 and she 19?" Vicky asked, Alessia laughed. Brenda interrupted "yeah but they look good together, check this picture out." Vicky sat down next to Brenda and looked at the picture of the celebrity couple standing together at a movie premiere. "Well, as long as they're happy I guess" Vicky said.

The trio carried on chatting about the latest celebrity gossip before Vicky interrupted them "have you ever thought what it would be like to meet a vampire?" Emily replied "no, why would you want to do that, they'll only bite you and suck out all your blood." Vicky remained unconvinced "I know vampires exist and they're trying to get rid of all of them, but what if they converted you into one instead of killing you, you would then live forever." Brenda replied "my dad hates vampires, when he was on holiday in Japan, there was an underground vampire colony near one of the tourists' resorts, some tourists were captured and killed by the vampires so the Japanese military attacked and killed them all. I think in a few years all the underground vampire colonies will be destroyed."

"Why do you want to live forever?" asked Alessia, "are you some sort of closet vampire like Janine? Everyone knows she has totally lost it." Vicky answered hesitantly "no, I'm curious that's all." Alissia sensed Vicky's hesitancy and joked "you look more like a vampire than Janine or any of us, they'll love your pale skin, dark brown eyes, long black hair and…." "fuck off okay, I ain't no vampire" Vicky uttered angrily as she got up, "I'm going to my room."

Emily beckoned to Vicky as she started to walk away "you want me to come by for a little, we can work on our presentations?" Brenda looked over to Emily and grinned "Emily you're such a slut, do you have to make it that obvious?" Emily blushed and replied vehemently "lay off Brenda, you're such a bitch!" Emily got up and followed Vicky out of the cafeteria.

They walked together down the hallway and up the stairwell leading to their dorm room floor. Emily still felt embarrassed "V, about what Brenda said, I mean.." Vicky smiled "That's okay, Brenda is a bitch. You can hang in my room for a bit but not for long as I'm really knackered." "Cool!" Emily replied now sporting a broad smile.

Vicky locked her dorm room door once Emily entered. She reached inside the wardrobe and took out the carrier bag with the artefacts. "M, have a look at the scroll, it has a figure on it that looks scary," Vicky put on her desk lamp and proceeded to unroll the scroll at her desk. "Ha ha, it looks like you!" Emily laughed while Vicky looked sullen "I was afraid you'd say that, that was exactly what I thought." Vicky walked towards the door "I'm going to the loo, I'll be back in a bit" Vicky unlocked her door and walked towards the communal toilets.

Emily peered at the scroll and began scratching it with her right index finger to see if the figure would fade. Nothing happened, the more she looked at the figure the more she felt it was alive and looking back at her. As she moved backwards the figure's eyes shifted to follow her movement. Emily fell backwards onto the bedroom floor; she trembled in fear before getting up and quickly rolling up the scroll, putting in the carrier bag and turning off the desk light.

"What happened?" asked Vicky as she returned from the toilet, "the scroll is scary, I felt it was looking at me" said Emily uneasily. "What did you see?" Vicky asked impatiently, "the figure's eyes followed me when I moved, it seemed like it was alive and looking at me." Vicky shuddered "M, let me see, this is important," Vicky switched on the desk light and unrolled the scroll, the figure didn't move. "I can't see it move M" said Vicky disheartened.

Emily replied fervently "I know what I saw, it really did come alive. Those artefacts are scary, you should get rid of them, I reckon they're haunted." Vicky nodded in agreement. Emily continued "Let's leave them and go work on our presentations, I'm not going to get a chance tomorrow." Vicky brought out her laptop and took down her bulky anthropological textbooks as Emily took out her textbook and notepad.

After fifteen minutes, Emily scratched her head and exclaimed "evolutionary anthropology is boring, I just can't focus; I think I need a hot bath instead." "C'mon M, you keep doing this, you're the one who wanted to study right?" Vicky said infuriated by Emily's scatterbrain antics. She turned her head to see Emily looking longingly at her, "maybe we should call it an early night, I'm really tired and can feel a slight headache coming on" said Vicky yawning.

Emily gestured towards her shoulders "I think I've injured my shoulder from carrying those heavy backpacks earlier, I've got this really good oil for it though, can you..." This was not the first time Emily had feigned a muscle injury in order to get a massage from her "I'll do it tomorrow M, I'm really tired" Vicky said sternly. "Pleaaasse, it will only be five minutes" Emily beseeched. "Not tonight M," Vicky said curtly.

Emily frowned "I love you Vicky" she said as she got up, putting her textbook and notepad into her bag before walking towards Vicky's dorm door "I love you too" said Vicky. Emily unlocked the door and turned towards Vicky "I just wish you would love me the same way I love you, you mean everything to me Vicky, you are...""Gud night M, you mean everything to me too" Vicky said smiling. Emily managed a tense smile as she closed the door behind her.

Vicky put away her laptop and textbooks and took out the scroll from the carrier bag and laid it out on her desk, she pulled out her desk chair and sat down to look more closely at the figure. As she peered closer her body become lighter and her breathing began to slow, she looked around her room and everything seemed normal. She assumed her light headedness was triggered by a lack of food.

She looked again at the scroll and this time she fell right back into her desk chair. The chair had become a magnet that gripped her like a vice. Vicky was frightened, she screamed as loud as she could yet nothing audible was heard. She tried desperately to close the scroll but she couldn't move her hands.

Then she heard a voice in the distance, it seemed far away but appeared to be gradually getting closer. She listened intently in order to make out what was being said but she could not decipher the feint words. As the voice got closer, the figure on the scroll started to metamorphasize into a three dimensional holographic face that resembled hers. She tried frantically to move but her limbs felt like they were stuck to her desk chair.

Vicky felt dizzy and closed her eyes. The room began to spin and smell of sulphur. Again she shrieked as loud as she could but still nothing came out. As she opened her eyes, the holographic face smiled "yooou arrrr nyyyzzz, yooou arrrr nyyyzzzz." She mouthed the words "what is nyzzzzzz?" but nothing came out or at least whatever she said was not audible within her range of hearing. The holographic face smiled and grew, Vicky trembled in shock, eventually it stopped growing.

Vicky looked up to see a holographic image of herself. The hologram was kitted out in her favourite Ugg boots, Birkin bag, Louis Vuitton scarf and Chanel earrings and pendant. Vicky twisted and turned and tried to get out of the chair. The hologram jumped down from the desk and stood next to Vicky, she whispered "shhhhhhhhhhhh" and as she did Vicky felt drowsy, the room began to spin again and this time she blacked out.

Vicky awoke the next morning to find the sun beaming through the gaps in the curtains. She looked around and saw no trace of the scroll, the holographic face or any sign of disturbance. She hoped that it was all just a really bad nightmare and that she could continue with her ballet class that afternoon as normal. She drew the curtains and looked out across the horizon, she longed to head home to see her parents in Brighton and spend time by the sea.

She got up, showered and brushed her teeth before grabbing her mobile phone and texting Emily "M, r u awake? Can I cum ova for a bit b4 breakfst, got2tell u about the crazie dream I had last nite xxx"

She took out her favourite jeans, designer t-shirt and jacket. After changing and applying her favourite make up, she checked her mobile. No response from Emily, if Emily was awake she would have responded already. But Sundays was Emily's lie in day and no one ever saw Emily emerge from her dorm room until after 11am.

Suddenly there was a knock at the door; Vicky rushed to open it believing it to be Emily. Instead, a tall, dark and handsome stranger dressed all in black stood there. He wore a bespoke black suit and had dark sunglasses and a black cowboy hat; he seemed to be around thirty with chiselled facial features. Vicky gasped, the stranger looked slowly at Vicky and smiled "aren't you going to invite me in? I've waited many hundred of years to see this day, the least you can do is invite me in!" Vicky opened the door and the stranger walked in.

He wore the latest Armani au du toilette and walked with a sense of conviction and purpose. Without being asked he pulled out the desk chair and planted himself on it "better lock that door, there is something I need to tell you" Vicky couldn't think, she locked the door and turned to face the stranger. "My name is Lorenzo and I'm from Napoli. I am one of the last" he paused "the last vampire guardians of the secret about the chosen one, about you."

Vicky listened intently, Lorenzo pointed to the bed "please sit down, I don't mean to impose." Vicky walked to her bed and sat down. "About five hundred years ago there was a war between humans and vampires, our kind lost and we were pursued relentlessly from country to country, from city to city, from house to house until few of us survived. And those that did so survived in underground colonies, living a horrible and godforsaken life."

"Now the final battle is about to commence, the humans have found ways to locate and destroy the last of our kind. The only thing standing between them and our destruction is you my dear, you are the chosen one, chosen to win the battle for us and with it our survival." He paused, giving Vicky a moment to digest what he had just said. "I am here to protect you, I will do whatever you ask of me my dear, please do not be afraid of me."

Vicky looked at him intently "will I be converted?" she asked. "If that is in your destiny my dear, one day you may be immortal but that is enough for now, in time you will discover all you shall need to know, in time..." "What about now?" Vicky asked. "The humans have deciphered some of our communiqués; they have a hit squad searching for you as we speak, two of my close friends who guard the secret were slaughtered a week ago. They are hoping one the guardians will lead them to you."

Vicky looked to the floor, tears filled her eyes and slowly began trickling down her pale cheeks, she knew life would never be the same again, for the first time she could actually feel the pain and suffering of the stranger. She knew that it would be unlikely that she would see her parents and her friends again. She felt twenty-one going on sixty rather than twenty-one going on twenty-two. Lorenzo spoke softly "please do not cry my dear, we must move quickly, there is little time. Please pack what you need, there will be supplies at the resthouse." "But I didn't want to be the chosen one, why can't things go back to how they were?" Vicky said sobbingly.

"My dear, that is what I want also, to go back to how things were long ago, when humans and vampires lived peacefully side by side, when our kind was not hunted like animals to the brink of extinction. But... alas that is not to be, today we must fight, fight for our survival, fight for a better tomorrow, fight for a future when we can live again in peace."

Vicky wiped the tears from her face, she turned burying her face in her pillow and wailed softly. "My dear, I am sorry" Lorenzo said dolefully. Vicky clenched her right hand and began pounding the mattress. Her wailing got louder, the pillow no longer muffling her cries. "My dear, someone may hear, we must go immediately and must not be seen." Vicky turned round, her eyes red from the tears, "just pack a few things, leave behind all electronic instruments and any mobile phones you have, they can trace it by satellite," said Lorenzo gently.

Vicky packed her contact lens, make up and toiletries. She folded a few blouses, tops and jeans and put them into her travel holdall. She looked at Lorenzo and nodded. He smiled and got up from the desk chair he had planted himself in when he arrived and beckoned to her "my dear, let us travel like the wind."

He walked to the door closely followed by Vicky, as she turned and locked her dorm door she felt a deep sense of grief. It was like her old self and everything she knew up to this point had died. And in front of her lay a whole new life. What the future would bring she did not know but she was about to find out.

The Transplant Surgeon

Alice had enough of Paul's infidelity, she would no longer put up with his lies and false promises. Paul had admitted to eight liaisons with unnamed women during their relationship, most of them occurring when he was away on business. He would always promise Alice that it was a one-off and a mistake and that it would never happen again. Alice crumbled and felt dejected each time it happened but she was willing to forgive him and give him another chance hoping he would somehow change his ways. She was tired of being taken for granted, she felt like a coat hanger in Paul's wardrobe, always there for him whenever he needed her.

She read of a new event in Time Out, it was called 'Encounters.' Alice heard about introduction agencies but had never seriously thought about giving it a go. Encounters used the latest astrological and personality tests to find a suitable partner, registration was limited to professionals of a certain pedigree. They demanded utmost disclosure on current relationships and prohibited long term serial daters. The registration event offered participants the chance to 'experience a whole new phenomenon in soul mate matching.'

Alice knew what she was going to wear to the registration night; she chose her favourite black skirt, striped blouse and designer leather jacket. As she ventured out from her apartment into the fresh London air she felt a sense of anticipation mixed with a degree of trepidation. She arrived at Green Park station at 8.00 pm and went straight to the venue.

From a distance the venue looked quite impressive, it was a big imposing building, six storeys high, with a lavish carpeted entrance and concierge. She went through the revolving doors to the reception desk and spoke to a friendly receptionist who directed her to the second floor. She was met by an elegant and well dressed woman in her early fifties who introduced herself as Candice, a mentor at Encounters. She was every bit the professor type, with spectacles and shadows under her eyes that suggested a little too many days burning the candle at both ends.

Candice led Alice into the waiting room before offering her a drink, though not thirsty Alice politely requested sparkling mineral water. A few minutes later Candice returned with the mineral water, Alice took the glass and began sipping the water. Candice sat next to her and asked "Alice, I know from your pre-registration questionnaire that your blood group is O+, that you are in good health and that you have no known medical conditions, is that correct?" Alice was taken aback at the focus on her medical history and jokingly replied "actually I do have a medical condition, I always attract men who treat me like a coat hanger, so I admit, I must have some sort of medical condition."

Candice laughed "it is not you who have a medical condition, it is men. I understand your situation, I have spoken to hundreds of women who are searching for a charming, intellectual and caring man who will treat them right. A man who will happily commit to a serious relationship rather than constantly engage in multiple short term relationships." "Exactly" exclaimed Alice, thinking she had finally found another woman who understood her predicament and her perspective on the modern man.

Candice spoke a little about her previous relationships and how she was now happily married to a surgeon who specialised in organ transplantation. Alice let her mind wonder for a second, the thought of being whisked off her feet by a dashing organ transplant surgeon was quite appealing.

Candice and Alice carried on chatting, Alice talked about her job and how she was happy with it even though at times she sometimes felt undervalued. After a good twenty minutes of banter, Candice started becoming fidgety, Alice noticed Candice's uneasiness but overlooked it. Candice asked "did you keep to the confidentiality agreement?" Alice paused to think "you mean the pre-registration form that requires me not to disclose to anyone that I am coming here tonight? All very James

Bond isn't it?" Candice laughed "we have our reasons you know." Alice responded "well I didn't tell anyone, in fact I wished I had told Paul, my current boyfriend. At least he would have got the hint."

"Good" Candice exhorted, "how is the mineral water, do you want some more?" Alice looked at the quarter full glass of mineral water sitting on the table besides her comfy brown leather chair; she reached over and gulped down what remained. "Or would you like to try a glass of our house red wine? We will be delivering a case to you as a thank you for using our services" Candice said smiling. "A little red wine won't go amiss" replied Alice as Candice smile broadened as she got up "great, I won't be a moment." Candice disappeared along a well lit corridor as Alice stretched out her arms in the air and let out a large yawn, the initial nervousness of coming to an introduction agency now wearing off.

Candice came back with a glass of red wine and directed Alice to follow her into an adjacent room. It was a large and very bright room; there was a conference table in the middle with a set of printed documents, two laptop computers and what looked like a mini-satellite on one side. They both sat down near the laptops. Candice entered some details onto the laptop and then turned to Alice "here is a little online survey I would like you to fill out, please be as honest as you can, everything is confidential here. As long as you are a member of Encounters your information will be kept safely and securely and we will not divulge it to any third party whatsoever."

Alice felt satisfied by Candice's assurance but started wondering when she would get the chance to meet all the potential soul mates that Candice had so enthusiastically talked about. "What is the next stage after this?" Alice asked. "Once we upload your information, we will then find you a suitable match and I will run through a few profiles with you" Candice relied. "That sounds good" exclaimed Alice.

"When you have finished press the buzzer next to the laptop and I will be back" Candice said as she pointed to the buzzer before walking out of the room in a hurry. Alice began filling in the survey, most of the questions were straightforward, asking her for information on her age, address, job, religion, past relationship history and partner preferences. The medical information and medical history section took up over half the survey making it seem more appropriate for medical insurance purposes than for an introductions agency. Thirty minutes later the form was complete. She rang the buzzer to let Candice know she had finished.

Candice returned to the room five minutes later and explained to Alice that her details were already being processed and the system had returned a few potential matches. She logged on to the laptop and began typing; Alice clasped her head with one hand, she felt quite light headed and a little dizzy. "Are you all right Alice?" Candice queried. "Yes, I just feel slightly light headed" replied Alice feebly. "Oh, I will get you some more water" Candice said and got up and walked hurriedly towards the door before Alice had a chance to object.

Alice put her head down to rest on the conference table. Candice came back with a jug of water and another glass, "here Alice, have some more water, I'm sure you will feel better soon." Alice struggled to sit up while Candice poured her a glassful of water. She gingerly grabbed the glass and took a sip. "Let me show you the matches our system has come up with" Candice opened a few windows and entered some information onto the laptop before turning the screen to face Alice.

She pointed to the profile of a man in his late fifties "this is Charles from Houston, he is looking for an O+ person in vibrant health with fully functioning kidneys." Alice began to feel more nauseous and put her left hand across her stomach and her right hand on her forehead. She spoke softly "I thought they would be in their thirties and from the UK?" Candice responded "it must have been a long week for you. Let me show you Victor, he is from Louisiana, he is in his early sixties and is looking for a suitable liver match." "Liver match!" exclaimed Alice "what type of organisation is this?"

Candice smiled sinisterly "we supply organs to the rich and wealthy and you are in high demand. We have had bids in excess of one million dollars for your liver." Alice felt as though she was going to vomit, she struggled to get up but she was too light headed. She felt for her mobile phone, luckily it was still in her jacket pocket, she pulled it out and dialled 999.

Candice looked pityingly at Alice, Alice pressed the dial button as Candice shook her head from side to side "I'm sorry Alice, we have blocked all mobile phones signals. Don't worry, you won't feel a thing, I promise." She patted Alice on her shoulder and got up to leave the room. Alice felt paralyzed, she turned to see where Candice was going, her head moving only a few centimetres but her eyes followed Candice towards to door.

Candice opened the door and in walked three men, two looked like security personnel and the other wore a smart white doctors uniform and carried a small rectangular case. He came straight up to Alice, put the case on the conference table and opened it. "Hello Alice, I am Alex the anaesthetist, I am so pleased you have joined our organisation, you are in good hands now." Alice sat slumped in the chair, her head tilted to the right, she could not move her head but her eyes darted across the room as she watched Alex and the two security personnel in front of her

Alex reached into the case and pulled out a syringe. Alice whimpered "nooooo" and struggled to get up. He nodded to the two security personnel who then walked over to Alice, ripped off her leather jacket and rolled up the right sleeve of her striped blouse. Alice continued to struggle as best she could but she was paralyzed by the drug she imbibed in the mineral water she was given.

One of the security personnel took a compression rope from the rectangular case and tied it around Alice's upper arm allowing Alex to inject her with an anaesthetic. Alice's eyes darted from side to side, she kept telling herself to stay awake but gradually she felt an overwhelming tiredness spread over her body and her eyes lid slowly began to droop. She tried to fight the anaesthetic but it was no use, she drifted into unconsciousness and regretted ever wishing to have a dashing encounter with an organ transplant surgeon.

The Rickshaw Wallah

Manoj was a rickshaw wallah who worked in the heart of Old Delhi. He arrived in the Indian capital six months ago from Zaihla, his home village in Haryana, two hundred miles away. Manoj had found the initial transition to city life difficult yet he had clung on to his dream of making it big. He headed to Chandni Chowk, a sector of Old Delhi full of bazaars, merchants, vagrants, dacoits and others. He knew immediately that life was going to be a daily battle and that only the fittest would survive.

The street Manoj had settled in was a den of depravity, overflowing with squalor, dust and debris. For the gangs and thieves of the area, Manoj was like a newly born sheep that had entered the wolves den.

Ashok, a street vendor who had lived in Delhi for the past five years befriended Manoj and took him under his wing. Manoj stayed in Ashok's apartment and ferried Ashok around the city for free in return for subsidized rent.

Ashok paid monthly protection money to Zair, the leader of the local Hauja mafia. But Zair was not happy; the local Barista café owner had not paid him any money for the last two months. The defiance by the Barista café owner and his vocal opposition to local mafia meant those who regularly paid protection money were also refusing to pay or paying later and less than before. An example had to be set, Ashok was friends with Bhatia, the café owner and on the request of Zair, Ashok invited Bhatia to dine with him at the exclusive Jasmine restaurant in Connaught Place.

As Bhatia and his wife Shena left their house to attend the dinner engagement, they were shot by Faisal, the Hauja mafia's hit man.

Once Ashok heard of the incident, he went immediately to Zair to get answers. Zair was nonchalant "examples have to be set, it was the only way." "Why not let me convince them instead?" asked Ashok. "No use" said Zair flatly "they would not have listened."

Ashok's weakness was his love of gossip, he began telling everyone he met at his stall the next day and everyday after that what Zair had done to his friend Bhatia, despite repeated warnings from Zair not to. Gossip was a way of life for the street vendors and rickshaw wallas, it made the day go quicker and easier and made their lives more bearable. It was a social practice that would cost Ashok his life.

Manoj was concerned about Askok's lack of restraint, he had warned him daily for ten days straight not to talk about the incident with Bhatia. Manoj feared Zair may kill him at any moment.

After closing his stall Ashok always returned promptly to the apartment he shared with Manoj. When Ashok didn't return one evening, Manoj knew something was wrong. He went to where Ashok's stall was and found it shut.

Manoj decided to go to Zair for help. As soon as he saw Zair he pleaded "Ashok is upset, he doesn't know what he says, he has started drinking again, please Zair, do give him a chance. He is a hard working street vendor, better than most and he always pays you monthly on time." Zair look and smiled "I know you care for your friend but to survive we need strict discipline, even Ashok knows that. I'm afraid Delhi has one street vendor less." Manoj went outside Zair's residence and dialled Ashok's cell phone, there was an automated message by the telephone operator stating the number he had dialled was no longer in service. He immediately returned to his apartment but there was still no sign of Ashok. Manoj inquired with the other street vendors and rickshaw wallahs but none of them had seen Ashok that day.

Manoj was distressed, he knew Ashok was dead. He was desperately sad that he didn't have a chance to say goodbye to his friend and couldn't even ensure he received the appropriate funeral rites.

The next day the local newspaper included a paragraph on the stabbing of a local street vendor in Chandni Chowk. Manoj kept the page in his drawer in memory of his friend.

The Prince of Atlantis

Once upon a time in the underwater kingdom of Atlantis there lived a prince called Fyodor. He was the only child of the elderly king and queen of Atlantis. It was time for the prince to find a bride and get married. Queen Amelia had chosen a suitable bride for Fyodor, she was intelligent, beautiful and very witty. But Prince Fyodor wasn't happy, so the queen gave him three months to find a suitable bride or get married to Dolcine, the bride she had chosen.

In his heart, Prince Fyodor wanted to find a bride from the Kingdom of Yerrus, a land located in the north far from Atlantis and beyond the cold and icy frontier. When he was younger he saw a picture taken by an explorer from Atlantis of young women dancing in Yerrus. Instantly, he fell in love with their long blonde hair, sparkling blue eyes and very fair skin. When he told his tutor Arcan how he felt, the tutor immediately rebuked him "that is not the way of our people, it is against tradition. You are a prince of Atlantis, you must take a bride from Atlantis." The prince listened to his tutor's admonition but his heart told him otherwise.

The prince explained his predicament to Idoris, Atlantis' most famous and most experienced explorer who travelled to Yerrus many years ago. After much deliberation, it was decided that a group of fifteen of Atlantis' best explorers and warriors would set forth to Yerrus with the prince and his aides to help him find the bride he longed for.

Two weeks after they set off and after much ordeal, the group arrived in the surprisingly warm, green and leafy kingdom of Yerrus. The group hid in the trees and observed how the people of Yerrus dressed and spoke. The prince sent two explorers to a local village to find them suitable local attire and another two to find a place for them to lodge.

Once changed the group went to the Inn House. The Innkeeper looked uneasily at the group as they entered the premises. Sensing the tension, Idoris stepped forward and offered the Innkeeper the finest jewels and gem stones from Atlantis. The Innkeeper smiled and waved the group along "you shall have my finest rooms and finest port" he chuckled.

Idoris knew that time was short, they had under two months to find the bride the prince longed for and to travel back to Atlantis through the treacherous cold and icy frontier. Early the next morning Idoris set off in search of Mandalay, a friend he met on one of his previous expeditions to Yerrus. He found Mandalay still living in the house on the hill, after much rejoicing they both sat down and Idoris explained the group's task. Mandalay leaned back on his finely engraved wooded chair and bellowed "not to worry great Idoris, many a young maiden from Yerrus would wish to marry the prince of Atlantis. Tomorrow we shall get to work."

The prince, Idoris and the rest of the group arrived early the next day at Mandalay's residence. Mandalay busily began giving instructions to each member of the group. They all set off in different directions, touring the local villages and town halls and spreading the news. By the evening, there was a queue of prospective brides outside the Inn House where the group lodged. The prince was shocked, he didn't expect the news to travel so fast.

He spoke to each prospective bride before going back to his room crestfallen. "What's the matter young prince?" asked a bemused Idoris. The prince looked up, his eyes filled with tears "all the women are beautiful but they do not love me at all, they only love my wealth and status. It is as my tutor Arcan told me long ago, I must find a bride from Atlantis. Let us return home tomorrow."

Idoris went to his room, sat down and thought. He wondered how he could find a bride from Yerrus who would love the prince for who he was and not because of his royal lineage or wealth. He had an idea but needed Mandalay's help. The prince would be disguised as a local, that way no-one would realise he was really a prince. Idoris rose early the next morning and went straight to the prince's room, before the prince could speak Idoris said resolutely "Give me a few days and if you do not find a bride by then, we shall return home." The prince agreed.

Idoris went to Mandalay and told him of his idea. Mandalay laughed and exhorted "how noble of you Idoris to search for a bride for the prince who loves him for who he really is. I shall do my very best to help you." He took Idoris to the pantry floor of the town's bakery where many young women worked. Mandalay whispered in Idoris' ear "the prince shall work here as a pantry worker, he shall start this afternoon." Idoris wondered whether the prince would agree with Mandalay's proposal. He went back to the Inn House and told the prince of Mandalay's proposal. The prince agreed cheerfully "yes I am happy to be a pantry worker; at last I may find my bride."

It took the prince two full days to get used to the rigours of the pantry floor, by the third day his body was accustomed to the new routine. On the evening of the fourth day the prince told Idoris about a pantry worker called Isobel. Idoris was overjoyed when the prince told him how warm, friendly and caring she was; and most of all how she liked the prince for who he was and not because of his wealth or status. Idoris instructed the prince to ask Isobel to dine with them at the Inn the following night.

The next day at the bakery the prince felt nervous; eventually he plucked up the courage to ask Isobel to join him for dinner that evening at the Inn. When she accepted the invitation he was elated. He jumped around the factory floor with glee.

After the meal, Idoris approached Isobel and told her the truth. Initially she was shocked but then agreed to come with the prince back to Atlantis. Back in Atlantis, the prince introduced Isobel to the king and queen. They were very happy that the prince had found a bride he loved. The royal wedding was arranged and there was twelve days of celebration. The prince and his Yerrus princess lived happily ever after in Atlantis.

The Magical Sea Shell

There was once a boy who lived by the sea. He was too poor to go to school so each day he wandered along the beach looking for treasure. Sometimes he found rusty one rupee coins, other times he found discarded car parts.

His mother used to tell him he was a nuisance, she had eight other children to feed and poor Vivek was always eating more than his share. He felt sad, he didn't want to be a nuisance so he walked miles everyday earnestly searching for gold and hidden treasure along the beach.

His grandfather Ravi saw the dejection on Vivek's face "now Vivek, don't be sad, you will find the treasure you are looking for one day. Keep on looking and one day..." Vivek's mother heard what was being said and interrupted abruptly "stop feeding his head with talk of treasure, he should go and work in Shenoy's factory like all the other kids." Vivek turned and walked out of the makeshift shack that was his home.

He wandered through the alleyways until he found the path that led to the beach. He walked slowly, his shoulders slumped and his head pointing to the ground. Eventually he reached the beach and sat on his favourite rock.

He looked out to sea and at the setting sun. He wanted to swim away and find a new life. Then he heard a dog bark and looked around, it was Arjuna the stray mongrel "Arjuna go away, I want to be on my own" Vivek shouted. Arjuna pricked up his ears and gave Vivek a puzzled look, then he turned and continued sniffing for food. As Vivek looked at the waves lashing against the sea shore and melting into the sandy beach he heard Arjuna bark again.

He looked round to see Arjuna digging away furiously with his two front paws. Vivek knew Arjuna was a wily old dog with a sense of adventure. A few months ago Arjuna's hind legs were injured by dacoits, instead of being scared or disheartened

Arjuna instead growled aggressively and looked directly into the dacoits eyes, making them flee with fear.

Vivek was curious to see what Arjuna had found so he walked over to where Arjuna was digging and shouted "Arjuna, what have you found?" Arjuna was too busy digging to bother with Vivek's shouts so Vivek knelt down and saw what looked like to be half eaten chicken bones, an old crisp packet and a sea shell. Vivek picked up the sea shell and held it up to the sun, it seemed to emit an orangey glow. He cleaned it in the sea before walking back to sit on his favourite rock, leaving Arjuna to feast on the chicken bones he had found.

He again held the sea shell up to the fading sun light and this time he could make out a series of grooves along the outer shell. Then he heard a strange sound, it was the wind blowing through the shell. He listened again and heard what sounded like an elephant's roar. He put the large side of the shell to his ear and listened but this time he heard nothing. It seemed that he would only hear the sound when air blew through the shell. So Vivek put the narrow side of the shell to his mouth and blew as hard as he could, puffing out his cheeks in the process.

Initially he heard nothing, then he heard the roar of elephants far away in the distance. He looked out to sea and saw nothing, he turned and looked back to shore and saw Arjuna sitting and relaxing on one side of the beach and a group of children playing cricket on the other side of the beach. The roar gradually began getting louder, it sounded like a herd of elephants was stampeding towards him. Vivek got up and turned to run back home when suddenly he was lifted into the air. When he looked back down again he found himself sitting atop of an adult female Indian elephant.

Vivek was scared, Rani, the elephant he was sitting on spoke gently "do not be afraid, I am Rani, you called me and I have come to you." Vivek didn't know how to respond, he paused and then blurted out "where are you taking me?" Rani replied softly "nowhere dear child, I am the remover of obstacles, all who need help in their life call me and I come to their aid." Vivek thought for a few moments then asked "can you help me find gold and treasure, so my mum will not shout at me anymore?" "Of course, dear child" Rani replied "close your eyes and make your wish."

Vivek closed his eyes and wished for lots of gold and treasure. When he opened his eyes he found himself sitting back on his favourite rock. As he looked around he saw a fairly deep hole in the sand near to where he was sitting, he climbed off the rock and walked towards the hole. As he got closer he saw a twinkle coming from inside the hole. He stopped in amazement, the hole was filled with gold nuggets and a silk purple bag. He looked inside the silk bag and found diamonds, pearls and sapphires, Vivek was overjoyed. He put the silk bag in his trousers pocket and the gold nuggets under his t-shirt before tucking it into his trousers. He walked as fast as he could back home.

As he entered his home he screamed "Amma, I have found treasure! I have found treasure!" His mother was hand washing the children's clothes at the back of the house, when she heard Vivek's screams she came rushing "what son, what have you found?" Vivek took out the gold nuggets from under his t-shirt and the silk bag from his trousers and gave it to her. Him mother smiled in astonishment "may god bless you son."

From that day forth Vivek no longer wandered the beach looking for treasure, instead he and his elder siblings attended school. They no longer lived in a shack near the sea but in a large house near a lake. Vivek finally had the new life he longed for.

Vivek never forgot Rani the elephant, Arjuna the dog and the magical sea shell. He went back to the beach every month for the next year looking for the sea shell to call Rani and thank her. But there was no trace of the sea shell or of Arjuna, the wily dog.

The Kebab Shuffle

"C'mon mate, how long is that chicken shish gonna take?" Joe asked. "Will be ready in five minutes" Hasan replied. "Hurry it up will you" Joe shouted, his speech slurred from an evening drinking endless pints of alcohol. Leonid sensed the unease of Hasan and the other staff at the kebab restaurant. He looked around at the other customers; all were either drunk or near enough drunk. He felt a sense of pride, having drunk six pints of beer and two double shots of whisky; he felt sober enough to drive home even though the Road Traffic Act deemed he was not.

After eating his burger and chips Leonid waited in the queue at the taxi stand. All of a sudden he heard shouting and looked up, it was another fight. As he walked towards the melee to get a closer look he heard Joe shouting "get back in line, stop jumping the queue." Leonid went up to Joe and asked what was wrong. Joe told Leonid that he and his friend Chris were waiting in line for a taxi when a group of four teenagers had barged into the front of the line instead of waiting at the back of the queue.

Leonid went up to the four teenagers and asked softly but sternly "why don't you lot wait in line, just go to the back and there will be no trouble." Leonid stood his ground and looked at them intently, when the four teenagers realised Leonid was serious and that he wouldn't budge they all walked off.

They returned fifteen minutes later, Joe and Chris had now got their taxi home and Leonid was second in line. Suddenly Leonid felt a sharp pain in his lower right back and screamed in agony, he moved his right hand towards the area, it was wet. When he pulled his hand back and looked at it he saw it was covered in blood, he realised he had been stabbed.

As he looked back he saw the four teenagers running away, two of them looked back at him and raised their middle finger before continuing to run away. One of them threw a broken beer bottle to the floor, the weapon used to stab Leonid. Leonid began to feel nauseous and collapsed on to the floor clutching his lower back with his right hand.

There was a commotion around the taxi stand, some women waiting in the queue began screaming and others began shouting and pointing in the direction of the fleeing teenagers. As more people began to gather, a lady in her late twenties appeared and shouted "let me through, I have first aid training, can someone please call an ambulance?"

A man in his fifties responded "I have spoken to the emergency services, an ambulance is on its way." She knelt down next to Leonid and attempted to reassure him "you have been stabbed, but don't worry an ambulance is on the way. My name is Emily and I have done first aid training with St Johns Ambulance, I will do my best to help you until the ambulance arrives."

Emily proceeded to take napkins from her purse and press them around the wound on Leonid's back to try to stop the bleeding. Leonid started to shiver. Emily continued "you'll be okay, tell me about yourself, what is your name?" Leonid moaned in pain and uttered faintly "Leonid." "You have such a lovely name, where is it from?" Leonid replied "can't you stop the pain, I can't bear it, I feel so ill." "That's normal" Emily replied as she tried to reassure Leonid "your body is going into shock, just relax and focus on your breathing."

"Is the ambulance coming?" asked Leonid anxiously. Emily could smell alcohol on Leonid's breath "have you had anything to drink tonight Leonid?" "Yes, six pints of beer and two double shots of whisky" replied Leonid embarrassed at having to reveal exactly how much alcohol he had drunk that evening. "But it is nothing, I'm used to it, we drink like this all the time in Russia" Leonid exclaimed. "Ah, so you're from Russia?" Emily asked. She paused and pondered what to say next before continuing "what a beautiful place, my friend Jane went there when she was at university. I would like to go there also if I get the chance, it would be really amazing."

In the distance the sound of sirens could be heard, Emily looked towards where the sound was coming from and saw a police car and a police van heading in their direction. The police car parked near to where Emily was kneeling, PC Stanley came over to Emily and knelt down. Emily was still pressing onto Leonid's stab wound.

Before PC Stanley could speak Emily retorted "his name is Leonid and he has been stabbed, he was waiting in the taxi queue when there was a fight between two sets of youths. He went to break it up like any good Samaritan and the group of four youths causing the trouble left. But they returned and stabbed him." "Which direction did they go? Did you get a clear view of what they were wearing?" asked PC Stanley. Emily pointed "They took the road towards the river. They were wearing clubbing gear, they had long sleeve shirts and I think one had a designer baseball cap on."

PC Stanley's colleague PC Ortega then addressed Emily "are you medically trained love?" "No" Emily replied "but I have been a volunteer with St Johns Ambulance." PC Ortega interrupted "would you mind moving love, I will take over now" Emily got up and PC Ortega used a cold pack to press against Leonid's wound and secured it around him. She then took his pulse, finding it weaker than she had anticipated, she put Leonid in the recovery position and started asking him questions to keep him conscious.

PC Stanley began speaking into his police radio informing the police station of the potential suspects and Leonid's condition. As he was speaking he heard the sound of sirens and turned around to see an ambulance speeding towards them. As soon as the ambulance stopped, two paramedics jumped out and ran towards PC Ortega. PC Ortega told them of the stabbing incident and of Leonid's current condition.

Ray shone a light into Leonid's eyes to activate his pupil reflex and check that his oculomotor nerve was still intact. Leonid was conscious but his pulse had weakened and his breathing was rapid, his skin was now pale and slightly clammy. Ray went back to the ambulance to get the stretcher.

Jay, the other paramedic, began to press against the wound to stop the bleeding. Leonid asked earnestly "am I going to be all right?" Jay spoke in his most consoling voice "you will be fine mate, just relax, we are going to stabilise you and transfer you onto a stretcher." After stabilising Leonid, Ray and Jay lifted Leonid onto the stretcher and took him into the ambulance.

Emily rushed to the ambulance and confronted Ray "do you mind if I ride in the ambulance?" Ray asked "how do you know the victim?" Emily replied curtly "I don't but I was the first to help him and he spoke to me so I know a little about him." PC Stanley interrupted "I think it is best if you wait in the police car, I have to speak to you and get some more information on the suspects."

Emily wasn't happy, she wanted to go in the ambulance. PC Ortega could see Emily's discontentment "come with me dear I'll take you to the car." Emily turned to look at the ambulance, Leonid now had various machines connected to him to monitor his vital organs. Jay was sitting in the back of the ambulance with Leonid, he was busy fixing Leonid's intravenous line. Emily shouted out "will he be okay?" Jay looked up and saw the grave concern on Emily's face "yes he will, fingers crossed" he said trying to sound as convincing as possible.

Ray started up the ambulance and it sped away into the cold night its sirens blazing and its large blue lights flashing and lighting up the surrounding area. Emily was lost in thought and reflection. The deafening sound of the ambulance's siren and its flashing lights reminded her of the loud dance music and the iridescent strobe lighting of the club she was in just a few hours before, drinking cocktails and happily dancing and partying the night away with her friends. Yet here she was, having the worst night of her life so far. PC Ortega saw Emily's dejected stance and sullen look and said enthusiastically "come love, you did all you could, let's go to the car."

Meanwhile as the ambulance sped towards the hospital Ray turned to Jay and asked "how's our fella doing back there Jay, I don't want to lose anyone on shift tonight, what's the odds?" Jay replied solemnly "he's unconscious and fading fast. Sorry Ray, afraid this guy has the same chance of surviving as you have of winning the lottery this Saturday."

The Forest Fairy

Once upon a time there lived a white fairy, her home was hidden in the depths of the impenetrable forest of Polkaray.

She fluttered here and there, sitting on the branches of tall conifers. She passed her day by speaking with the rabbits, squirrels and birds. Some say the white fairy granted wishes to anyone lucky enough to speak with her. Others say she is the mother spirit of the forest, the guardian of all forest creatures.

One fateful August day, a little boy visited the Polkaray Park, on the outskirts of Polkaray Forest. He was on a day trip with his parents and they were all enjoying a quiet afternoon picnic. But little Peter was curious, he loved to explore the unknown. As his parents chatted amongst themselves about arranging the next annual family holiday and about buying a new family car Peter wondered away.

He ran, skipped and jumped and before long he was lost deep in the heart of the forest. But brave little Peter was happy, he was only concerned with finding a suitable tree to climb. Eventually he found a tree full of branches but without any leaves, he climbed halfway up the tree and looked around to see if he could figure out the route back to his parents.

In the distance he noticed a tree that sparkled, Peter rubbed his eyes because he wasn't sure whether the white glow he saw was real or an illusion. He climbed back down and walked in the direction of the white glow, as he came closer to the sparkling tree he stopped suddenly in his tracks.

The white fairy was sitting on a branch of the tree looking at him. Initially Peter was scared, but when he saw that the white fairy had a broad smile on her face he smiled back and asked "Are you real or am I dreaming?", the white fairy laughed hysterically and almost fell of the branch she was sitting on. "I'm the white fairy, the queen of the forest and who are you?" the white fairy asked. "I'm Peter from London and I'm here on a day trip with my parents. You look really small to be queen of this big forest, but if you are the queen, can you show me the way out of the forest and back to my parents?"

The white fairy smiled and said "close your eyes and turn around and you shall find the path back to your parents." Peter closed his eyes and turned around, he opened his eyes and saw white petals along the forest floor leading into the distance. Peter turned back to thank the white fairy but she had vanished along with the sparkling tree.

Peter followed the white petals until he came to an opening at the edge of the forest and saw his parents in the park running around and shouting his name. He walked calmly towards them, as soon as his parents saw him they rushed over. "Peter, I told you not to go wandering off without us" his mother shouted.

His father knelt down and began brushing Peter's shirt with his hands "what have you got all over your clothes, where did all this white glitter come from?" he asked. Peter looked down at his shirt and trousers "It was the white fairy" he explained "she is the queen of the forest, she must have put the glitter on me." Peter's parents looked cross.

"Peter, we're taking you home, I've had enough of all your make up stories justifying your so-called wild adventures" his father said, chiding Peter. "But it is true" Peter implored; "go to the car and wait" Peter's mother said pointing to where their car was parked.

As his parents went to gather their picnic hamper Peter rummaged through his pocked and found an old amulet given to him by his grandmother. He left it behind an old oak tree near the opening to the forest, on the edge of Polkaray Park. His grandmother had told him that the amulet had special powers and would protect him from danger and misfortune. He left it to thank the white fairy for helping him and hoped that the amulet would protect the white fairy and all the forest creatures.

Breaking News: The High School Mafia Update

By Larry Leno

North London Post, 10 June 2018

Kingsley Grove, the fee paying school in the leafy and affluent North London suburb of Highgate issued a statement yesterday confirming that from the beginning of the new school year there would be regular searches of students lockers, random drug tests and that a new exclusion policy will operate for any student caught using or possessing illegal drugs.

Phil Harvey, the deputy headmaster of Kingsley Grove who has taught at the school for the past twelve years stated "I never expected Kingsley Grove to be at the centre of an underground cartel that has spread to include other schools in London and the Home Counties."

Chris Harvey was at pains to stress that Kingsley Grove students have always achieved outstanding results at GCSE and A levels, last year the percentage of students achieving grade A-C in 3 A-levels stood at 93%. He seemed exasperated as he talked to the Post last month about the new breed of malevolence, nicknamed the 'high school mafia' and how Kingsley Grove became the centre of a police investigation into the death of teenager Yossi Berger.

Henry, an undergraduate student at Warwick University and former student at Kingsley Grove spoke to the Post about the rise of the mafia. "It all started with Marlo, he was a talented footballer but lacked any academic prowess. His brother Christian, the mastermind of the group, used to be a high-flying investment banker before turning to selling drugs. Marlo said Christian was convicted of supplying Class A drugs, mainly ecstasy, speed and cocaine.

Christian used to meet Marlo after school in his Porsche turbo and take him to football training at Arsenal Football Club. Everything went downhill when Marlo injured his right knee, he dropped out of Arsenal's youth academy and lost his place in the school's football team. Marlo began supplying drugs to his close friends, then as demand increased; he hired his classmates Dan and Ramone as dealers. Ramone was suspended once because of drug dealing but somehow he managed to continue dealing without any of the teachers knowing."

Another former student explained how the Kingsley Grove mafia operated "the scheme was sophisticated, a student had to be vetted before they could buy from Dan. This basically meant they had to be known to the dealers or their friends, or be part of the party scene. If Dan was suspicious, he would make them leave the cash in an envelope behind the grey lockers on the fifth floor of the art block at a certain time. Then the drugs would be left for them at another location in the school at a particular time. Dan always tried to avoid mobile and text usage, he preferred face to face communication or used coded handwritten notes on a note pad."

Marlo quit Kingsley Grove at sixteen after passing just six GCSEs, but he is understood to have taken overall control of the supply and sale of drugs at all the schools the mafia operated at, leaving the importation and overall control of the mafia to Christian. The mafia's illegal activities may have continued undetected for many years if it was not for the untimely death of Yossi Berger.

Yossi Berger's sixteenth birthday celebrations at his parents Golders Green home turned into a tragedy. The teenager decided to celebrate with friends and unfortunately for him, a lethal cocktail of drugs. He was known to take recreational drugs regularly, but on the night of his birthday he is understood to have taken five ecstasy tablets, a mixture of various alcoholic drinks and smoked copious amounts of cannabis. He was found by his best friend in the toilet slumped over the toilet bowl with vomit running down his face. The emergency services tried their best to resuscitate the teenager but he died later that night in hospital from water intoxification, hyponatremia, and cardiomyopathy.

The police investigations into the Kingsley Grove mafia continue. A statement issued by the Metropolitan Police earlier today confirmed that they have shut down the mafia's operations and have initiated investigations at all the schools where the mafia supplied drugs.

Police have also confirmed that they are investigating reports into other so-called 'high school mafia' groups that allegedly exist in London, the north-east and the midlands. Alarmingly, a group nicknamed the 'Notting Hill Mafia' are reported to be more sophisticated that the Kingsley Grove group, using couriers and advanced counter surveillance equipment. Police have also begun efforts to shut down the various 'high school mafia' fan group pages and blogs appearing on social networking sites.

Galactic Peacekeepers

By Nancy Oregon

Editor, New York International News

30 June 2215

Matthew 5:9 "Blessed are the peacekeepers, for they shall be called sons of God."

United Nations Security General Hernandez Da Silva announced earlier today at a hastily arranged press conference at the United Nations headquarters in New York that he had received a threatening communiqué from an alien race known as the Manicheans. The Security General refused to answer questions but promised to give further information on the communiqué at another press conference next week.

According to Magdalene Yarris, a researcher in Alien Life Forms at Princeton's prestigious Neptune Research Centre "the Manicheans live on the distant planet Solus V. Satellite images show Solus V to be very similar to the Earth in terms of climate, atmosphere and landscape, increasing the likelihood that there could be an intelligent life form similar to humans inhabiting this distant land. Over the last fifteen years we have noticed increased activity in the night sky, with various unidentified objects entering and leaving Earth's atmosphere. It is highly unlikely that this activity could be attributed to natural phenomenon and therefore, some scientists have suggested that the Earth is being visited by an alien species."

Sources in the intelligence and military communities have suggested that the destruction of the Earth's atmosphere and environment was the trigger for the Manicheans to send their elite forces of Mithraic knights to the Earth to gather information on a possible invasion plan.

Although the Manicheans are assumed to be benevolent galactic peacekeepers that travel the galaxies bringing harmony and balance to misaligned planetary systems, the Mithraic knights are quite different. They are elite Special Forces whose job is to defend and secure compliance with Manichean resolutions.

Ironically, 'Soka Gakkai', a book by author Callum Stalk predicted the invasion of the Earth by an alien race one hundred years ago. Soka Gakkai paints a terrifying picture of the Earth destroyed by environmental damage and being invaded by galactic peacekeepers who kill all humans as if they were locusts and then proceed to establish a protectorate to safeguard the Earth.

Stalk called these galactic peacekeepers the 'United Nations of the galaxy'. Initially these peacekeepers issued warnings to the United Nations asking them to take measures to stop the continual environmental destruction. But failure to reach consensus in the Security Council resulted in inaction.

The subsequent invasion of the Earth resulted in the massacre of all humans. Stalk's novel was undoubtedly influenced by his own life story; he lived on an island in the Pacific which was submerged due to rising sea levels from the melting of the polar ice caps. However, the uncanny similarities between Stark's novel and the world's current circumstances are too stark to ignore.

The Gardener

Asif grew up in Tooting, a diverse neighbourhood in South London. He was an ordinary boy who got ordinary grades at school. He seemed like just another average teenager who would follow a nondescript middle of the road path in life.

After studying art, history and sociology at A-Level, he became a mechanic. Over the next few years he dedicated himself to his job and eventually he was promoted to senior mechanic. He had a string of failed personal relationships with women he met at bars in London and developed a love for football and alcohol. His life was uneventful until the age of twenty three, when Mustafa entered his world.

He met Mustafa at his mid-weekly football training session on Tooting Common. Mustafa was tall and slim, he never drank alcohol and hardly ever spoke. Asif always avoided Mustafa thinking he was an unfriendly prude. One evening after training when the team went to the King's Head pub to unwind, Mustafa bought Asif two pints of lager, Asif reciprocated by sitting at Mustafa's table.

"Why don't you drink anything alcoholic?" Asif asked. Mustafa smiled and replied "I don't need alcohol to make me feel merry my friend, I am drunk in joy from belief, belief in the true god Gaia." Asif was stunned and a little intrigued, Mustafa seemed like an over zealous environmentalist.

Mustafa continued "can't you see, you are just a grain of sand on a beach with billions of others, just watch the film 'The Assassination of Richard Nixon' with Sean Penn, you will see what I am talking about." He paused before continuing "Why not become somebody, why not be that grain of sand that everyone remembers. For one moment you can have all the eyes of the world on you and only you, you have the potential to leave the world dumbfounded and awestruck."

Asif shifted around nervously in his chair and listened as Mustafa became more vociferous and animated. "We must be the proverbial gardener, the one who protects and nourishes his plants in all kinds of weather. We must not let weeds grow and take hold. Now that our very ecosystem is threatened, it is time to take a stand."

Asif paused wondering what kind of stand Mustafa meant "oh, you mean I should join Greenpeace or Friends of the Earth?" "Yes my friend" Mustafa said reassuringly, "listen to your heart, it will tell you what you must do." "I'd like to protect the Earth but I am just a mechanic, there is only so much I can do" Asif said.

Mustafa looked intently at Asif and spoke in a slow hushed tone "but what if you were chosen to save Planet Earth, to destroy the corporations and governments that have colluded in destroying the eco system?" Asif looked intently but slightly bemused at Mustafa, eager to hear what he had been chosen for. Mustafa could see the longing in Asif's deep brown eyes "you can choose to strike fear at the enemies' very core and bring fear into their hearts, you can be one of the magnificent saviours of the Earth, an Earth Warrior." Asif looked a little confused, his brow furrowed. Mustafa smiled and asked "Are you willing to take up the challenge of the Earth Warrior?" "Yeah sure" Asif earnestly replied.

Mustafa's language was vitriolic but his tone was soft so Asif eased back into his chair and relaxed, he had heard Mustafa speak like this before to Harry, the team's goalkeeper. He assumed this was more theorising and lecturing. Lying further back in his chair Asif exclaimed loudly "so I will have to attend rallies and join campaigns right?" Mustafa remained unmoved by Asif's remark, he continued using the same inflection "I can arrange for you to be sent to our training camp in Yemen for two weeks, you will learn the skills of the Earth Warrior and then you will return to the enemies' camp and set it on fire."

The whole idea of setting fire to things frightened Asif, he was a quiet and gentle person by nature even though his large frame and loud nature suggested otherwise. The thought of going to Yemen also did not appeal to Asif, if Mustafa had suggested Bondi Beach in Australia or Waikiki Beach in Hawaii he probably would have agreed.

Mustafa looked at Asif's bewildered expression and said reassuringly "don't worry, you will do great things, you will be remembered throughout history and the Earth will thank you for your good deed. Now go, don't tell anyone what we have spoken about until I see you next Saturday with instructions and details of your flight."

Asif was now concerned, he didn't realise he was expected to travel to Yemen so soon. "How long does this Earth Warrior training last?" he asked "not long Asif, not long" Mustafa said comfortingly, slapping his hand gently down on Asif's arm. Then he held Asif's arm tightly "go now Asif, time is short, I will see you next Saturday with instructions, god willing" Asif rose slowly and left the pub dazed.

Mustafa met Asif again at football training one week later. Mustafa smiled "are you ready for your training, we have the best instructors in the world?" "I don't think the whole Earth Warrior bootcamp training thing is for me, besides I have a job to do and I can't take holiday leave at such short notice" Asif replied.

Mustafa seemed to be expecting Asif's answer. "Do not worry, I have £1000 cash to cover you for the two weeks when you will be away. All you need to do is tell your employer that there is some sort of emergency and that you will have to be away for two weeks, can you do that?" Asif remained unconvinced "I'm really not the warrior type, you can save the £1000 and give it to Greenpeace, I'm sure they'll be able to do a lot more with the money." "Of course they could" Mustafa said, "but so far they have not stopped the environmental destruction, have they?" "No" Asif concluded.

"Do you want to let the Earth be destroyed or are you willing to take a stand?" asked Mustafa. Asif looked at Mustafa, he eyes seemed to penetrate his very soul. He felt a shiver down his back even though it was a warm summer's day. Asif replied forcefully "Look, I will call you tomorrow with the answer, now let's play football," Mustafa nodded in reply.

That evening as Asif watched a re-run of Eastenders, he thought deeply about the two weeks training and the chance of a holiday in Yemen. His work was boring and he hadn't had a holiday in two years. An activity holiday could be exactly what he needed. He picked up the phone and told Mustafa that he would be happy to go on the two weeks training course. To his surprise, Mustafa turned up at his front door within thirty minutes.

Mustafa greeted Asif's parents and went up to his bedroom. He took out a brown envelope and gave it to Asif "here is the £1000 cash," "thanks" Asif replied as he reached out to take it. "Your flight to Yemen is in two weeks, I will bring you the tickets and further details tomorrow. I know you have made the right choice, the Planet Earth will thank you for your sacrifice." Asif smiled, a two week activity holiday in a hot sunny country didn't seem like a big sacrifice.

Asif told his employer that he would need to go away for two weeks on short notice since his Uncle in Yemen was ill. Surprisingly, his employer agreed to his request. Asif told his parents and younger brother that he was going on an activity holiday, they all seemed pleased. Tariq, Asif's younger brother joked "remember to bring me back a present, preferably an attractive Yemenese girl." "Ha ha, very funny" Asif said mockingly.

The day of the flight arrived, Asif had packed all the items Mustafa had asked him to in his suitcase. He was apprehensive but looking forward to his trip. Hamid met Asif at Yemen's Sana'a international Airport; he was whisked away in an air conditioned Toyota Avensis to the Gaia Army training camp in the north of Yemen.

Asif was disheartened, there was no beach, no girls and everyone seemed very serious and uptight. Hamid led Asif to his bunk in the camp's dormitory, "you can rest for an hour, then Carlo will collect you and take you for training" he said unemotionally. Asif unpacked and lay on his bunk looking up at the ceiling fans, the faded curtains and the corrugated iron partitions.

He wondered if he had made a big mistake accepting Mustafa's offer. Later Carlo came and took him to the training ground. Carlo was a large muscular man with a thick guttural Russian accent. Asif found out later from Julius, a recruit from California, that Carlo was ex Russian Special Forces, apparently one of the best operatives the Gaia Army had.

Carlo trained Asif in basic hand to hand combat, basic surveillance and counter surveillance, espionage, technological and physical evasion and the use of explosives, specifically sophisticated roadside explosive devices. At the end of his first week's training, Asif was taken from the training camp to a heavily guarded house in the coastal city of Al Hudaydah.

Two armed men led him through the house, down some stairs and along a dimly lit underground corridor into an underground room. There was a well dressed man sitting at a desk typing on one laptop whilst looking at another laptop just next to it. He had two mobile phones and a bunch of keys laid neatly together on the desk.

He looked up as he saw Asif and his two armed minders enter the room. "Ah Asif" he exclaimed "welcome, welcome, I am Nizar, one of the Council members of the Gaia Army, please have a seat on the sofa there." Nizar pointed to the brown leather sofa on one side of the room. He then gestured to the two minders to leave the room before getting up from the desk and sitting next to Asif.

"Asif you have done well, you will soon be coming to the end of your training and I have decided to give you a very special task." He handed Asif a file that was sealed with red sealing wax and tied with a golden thread. Asif reached to open the file but Nizar interrupted "not yet, you must open this once you have finished your training." Asif nodded and spoke anxiously "How long will the task take, I have to get back to my job and my family and friends in London?" Nizar looked at the concern in Asif's face and tried to reassure him "not long Asif, about a month or so at best, Mustafa will take care of your family in London, he will tell your employer that you have been unexpectedly delayed."

Nizar lowered his voice and continued "do not worry, we will do everything we can for you and your family, you have my word." Asif felt reassured. He felt calmer as he was escorted back to the training camp.

That evening he met Julius at the camp's dormitory, it was only the second time he had met him. "How come nobody speaks English here?" Asif asked, "most people are locals or from Saudi Arabia and parts of east Africa, they do not understand English" replied Julius. "I didn't think the training would be so hard core, I was expecting more of a two week activity break. Now I have got this task from Nizar so it looks likely it will be another month or so before I can go home."

Julius knew what he had to do, he was planted by Nizar to reassure and prepare Asif for what was to follow. "I had a task, to kill Phil Carter and Turner Young, two of the outspoken critics of Gaia belief and committee members of the American Climate Change Panel. It wasn't as easy as I thought it would be but I did the task. Don't worry, the Gaia Army will be with you ninety per cent of the way, all you have to do is go that final mile on your own."

Asif looked worried, he didn't want to kill anyone. "What if I can't do the task or I decide to quit and go home?" Asif asked anxiously, "they pick a task that you are capable of so you should be fine" replied Julius. "Once you are part of the Gaia Army you can never leave, Harris came over from Manchester three months ago, he didn't like his task and wanted to quit. I heard that the Gaia Army killed him, they told his family he died in a sky diving accident. Whatever your task is, you must do it or they will kill you. Then you can return home but you must never mention anything about the Gaia Army, the Council or your task."

Asif was speechless, he sat on his bunk frozen as if he had just looked into Medusa's eyes. Julius put his hand on Asif's shoulder "you should be happy, you are one of the very few chosen to be an Earth Warrior, you will be making a difference to the Planet Earth that will last generations."

Asif sat motionless, he face expressionless. "I have some locally brewed Sana'a beer and some khat, I'll be fifteen minutes" Julius said as he walked out of the dormitory and into the warm humid Arabian night. Twenty minutes later he returned with a blue carrier bag, he took out a bottle of beer, opened it and handed it to Asif.

Asif sipped it slowly, he was still in a state of shock. Julius sat in the bunk opposite him and opened a bottle of beer, he leaned back and took a few swigs. After ten minutes, Asif put the empty bottle down at the side of his bunk and lay down on his mattress. He stared at the ceiling motionless. Julius took out a wad of khat and left it on the table next to Asif's bunk, he turned to Asif "here is some khat, take some and chew it, after awhile you will feel its effect, it is like cannabis with a spike of speed." Asif didn't respond, he looked as if he was transfixed by something on the ceiling.

Julius sat looking at Asif and said a silent prayer, he got up and bid Asif farewell "I'm off now, my training requires me to go to Indonesia in three days, it is time that the Japanese Fisheries Agency change their policy on commercial whaling. If you need anything before then, speak to Hamid and he will let me know."

The next morning Asif rose at eleven, he was lethargic and had a slight hangover from the beer and the khat. Usually Carlo came to wake him at seven for a pre-breakfast drill so Asif felt a little concerned. Asif washed and strolled to the canteen, one the Yemenese instructors was sipping tea, Asif asked "have you seen Carlo?" the instructor replied in broken English "tomorrow, today rest, you Carlo tomorrow."

Asif had breakfast and went back to his dormitory bunk to think. He decided that he must open the file Nizar gave him even though Nizar had told him to wait until the end of his training. He got up, put the file and a bottle of still mineral water into a carrier bag and walked towards the dry riverbed on the outskirts of the training camp.

He sat down and slowly untied the golden thread before breaking the red seal. Inside the file he found pictures of a man in a suit, as he read the documents he realised the man was Carl Poulter, the chief operating officer of World Oil and Gas, the world's largest oil and gas conglomerate. A shiver went through his body as he read further; his task was to assassinate Poulter by planting a remotely activated road side explosive device along the route Poulter used regularly to travel to work.

He knelt forward and clasped handfuls of earth in each of his hands; he raised his hands to the sky and let the earth fall uniformly from both of his hands to the ground. He felt a jolt of electricity fly through him and fell backwards onto the gravel riverbank.

For the first time Asif felt really alive, not the feeling some people get when they accomplish the impossible but the feeling one gets when they realise that their own death may be imminent. He noticed things that five minutes ago he took for granted. He noticed how the ants at his feet were running along in what seemed to be some incomprehensible system and how pleasant the golden rays of the sun felt as they penetrated his skin.

He looked to the horizon and swallowed slowly, as if he was swallowing for the last time, savouring the beauty all around him. He took a deep breath then exhaled slowly as he glanced back to earth.

He stood up, threw his arms in the air and screamed until he could scream no more. Nothing comprehensible came out, it was a cathartic salutary goodbye to the beauty of life and of the world he once knew. Tears rolled down his face and his nose dripped with mucus.

He fell to the ground smashing his fists on the uneven gravel surface as hard as he could, he saw blood from his hands drip onto the ground but he did not feel any pain. He felt a sharp cutting pain deep inside his body; his heart was bleeding with anguish and sadness. He sobbed silently, not bothering to wipe the tears or mucus away from his face anymore, he felt so close to the Earth, the mother planet. He sat silently for ten minutes with his eyes closed, the rays of sun dancing on his eyelids.

When he opened his eyes again he was different, a changed man. Something inside of him had died and he was now reborn a new man, an Earth Warrior. He had finally accepted that he may have to sacrifice his life to ensure the survival of the Earth. He had become a convert and was ready for the task that lay ahead of him.

A Fortune Cookie

Lisa loved Chinese food, her favourite Chinese dish was sweet and sour chicken. The first time she tried Chinese food was at a restaurant in London's Chinatown with her former partner Craig. Sadly Craig was killed in a car crash not long after the meal as he travelled to Gatwick Airport on his way to a conference in Chicago.

Lisa's sister Hannah had arranged a birthday party for her on the last Saturday of June and had a surprise in store for her, she planned to introduce Lisa to Ben, her work colleague and an established chartered surveyor from Fulham. It was two year's since Craig's death and Hannah felt it was time for Lisa to get over her loss and move on with her life.

Lisa arrived at the plush Shanghai Express restaurant early and greeted everyone she was familiar with. She saw a tall, slim and handsome gentleman smiling at her, feeling slightly embarrassed she proceeded to introduce herself "hi I'm Lisa, have we met before?" "No we haven't, my name is Ben" he replied, "and I've heard a lot about you from Hannah." "Oh really" uttered Lisa, wondering what Hannah had been saying "what exactly has Hannah said about me?"

Ben sensed that Lisa probably thought Hannah mentioned something embarrassing or personal, given the fact that when their eyes first met he had a wry smile on his face. "Hannah just mentioned that you love Chinese food and that you enjoy travelling, she mentioned that you enjoy visiting Italy?" Lisa replied breathing a sigh of relief "I love everything about Italy, the food, the weather, the people and the beautiful language." Lisa's eyes sparkled as she spoke, talking about Italy made her feel jubilant "I've been there four times already, have you been to Italy before?" Ben smiled "Only once but I had an amazing time, I travelled from Venice to Rome." The Chinese waiter then ushered the guests to their specially prepared table.

The manager Charlie Wan came out and announced 'fortune cookies anyone?' a cheer went around the table and nearly everyone shouted 'yes' in tandem. Lisa was silent and Ben looked at her a little startled "you're not into fortune cookies are you?" "No" relied Lisa "I know it is all fun but sometimes I feel they might tempt fate." "Fair enough, let's avoid them then" insisted Ben. "No you go ahead, I mean it's probably me being silly as usual. I'm really interested in what your cookie says" said Lisa happily. Charlie began handing out the fortune cookies and everyone except Lisa reached out to take one.

Lisa looked on apprehensively as Ben ate the cookie and looked at the message. "So what does it say?" barked Lisa. Ben was still staring at the message "well...it says that my success lies in intellectual pursuits whereas danger lies in the fast lane!" Ben continued "these messages are so cryptic, I have absolutely no idea what it means." 'Lisa pondered over the message for a few seconds then said solemnly "I think it means you shouldn't go racing, have you ever gone racing?' "No but it is something I would love to do" replied Ben cheerfully.

The waiter brought out the hors d'oeuvre and the party started tucking into the sumptuous food. Ben and Lisa continued chatting, the more they got to know each other the more they liked each other. By the end of the night they had agreed to meet for dinner the following Saturday.

Ben decided to take Lisa to the Waterside Inn restaurant in Bray for their Saturday dinner rendezvous. Lisa spent the whole week wondering what to wear and spent hours on the phone to Hannah finding out more about potential suitor Ben. Lisa arrived at the venue and saw Ben waiting for her near the river, he was dressed in a smart charcoal grey Christian Dior suit.

Lisa felt like a teenager on a first date, the hairs at the back of her neck stood up and she had goose bumps on her arms and legs. Ben greeted her with a big kiss on the cheek and complimented her on her dress, it was a vermillion coloured Oscar de la Renta short sleeve dress and it perfectly matched her red Birkin bag and Christian Louboutin high heels. They sat down to dinner and Lisa marvelled at the wondrous array of dishes and the picturesque views of the Thames, it was like something out of book Wind In The Willows.

"I'm working on a new project at work, it's related to the London Crossrail scheme" said Ben as they sat down at the table he had reserved for them, "it's really complex so I have had to work overtime over the last week." "Sounds like you had a tough week?" replied Lisa. "Yes you could say that" said Ben with a big huff "my boss has been really putting the pressure on me, I have a public inquiry coming up on Monday and I have yet to prepare for it. Looks like I will be spending all of Sunday working." "Poor you" said Lisa smiling "sounds like you need a vacation."

Ben continued as if he did not hear what Lisa had just said "I have two meetings on Tuesday and I have to attend a planning appeals hearing on Thursday. I am totally snowed under at the minute. I feel a little guilty coming out tonight when I have so much work on my plate." Lisa was astonished; she looked at Ben to see if he was joking. Ben was still staring out the window "I don't get paid as much as I should you know, I do the work of two men, my salary should be double what it is now." Lisa's stomach churned, she excused herself and went to the toilet. She hoped Ben would snap out of his obsession with himself and his job by the time she returned.

As she returned to her table, she saw Ben busily typing on his Blackberry, "is everything okay?" she asked. "Yes, I just thought I would reply to a few emails while you went to the loo" Ben said as stared at the screen of his Blackberry. Lisa sat down at the table, "I just got an email from my colleague Francis" said Ben. "He has asked me to check out a Land Securities file on a retail park in Berkshire and a British Land file on a site in London. I can't believe how cheeky he is, trying to offload his work onto me. Did you know he takes a one and a half hour lunch break instead of the allocated one hour?" Ben said angrily.

"And sometimes he leaves work early to go off gallivanting around London or go on weekend breaks around Europe. It is just outrageous the gall of the man."

Ben continued throughout the entire evening to enlighten Lisa on the trials and tribulations of being a senior chartered surveyor at a large London firm. Lisa was not happy, what was supposed to be a romantic meal at a famous Michelin star restaurant was ruined by Ben's obsession with himself and his job.

Lisa drove home disappointed, she was attracted to Ben but they were not compatible. He needed a companion who would put up with his all consuming obsession with his job. Lisa phoned Hannah the next day to tell her the disappointing news. "Just give him another chance, he really likes you Lisa" pleaded Hannah, "he is always telling me at work how wonderful and how attractive you are." "Sorry Hannah" replied Lisa "we're just not compatible."

Over the next month Ben tried calling and texting Lisa several times a week but she avoided taking his calls and replied to his texts inviting her to dinner by saying she was busy. She hoped that eventually Ben would get the message that she was not interested.

On the August bank holiday weekend, Lisa invited Hannah over to her apartment for Sunday lunch. Hannah turned up just before midday at Lisa's swanky apartment overlooking Canary Wharf and the Thames. Hannah took out an odd looking figurine and put it on Lisa's lacquered sideboard, "it's from Ben" Hannah exclaimed "a present from Guatemala." "What is it?" asked Lisa. "Apparently it is a Guatemalan worry doll, you whisper your worries to it, place it under your pillow and when you wake up all your worries will have disappeared!"

"Nice theory, if only everything was as simple as that" said Lisa grinning "seriously Hannah, Ben has been calling and texting incessantly, he doesn't seem to get the message." Hannah chortled and asked "why not give him another chance? He really is a lovely guy." Lisa was lost in thought. "His birthday is next week and his brother Graham has booked him a trip to Silver Hatch. He would love for you to be there" said Hannah.

"I'm busy next week, but am free the following week. I just hope he doesn't end up talking about himself and his job again" replied Lisa jovially. "Ben told me what happened at the Waterside Inn, he said he didn't mean to be so selfish and self-obsessed. He had a bad migraine that day so it really was one of his off days" chuckled Hannah. As they feasted on salmon en croute and a dessert consisting of treacle sponge pudding and Haagen-Dazs ice cream they chatted about Ben, Hannah's forthcoming trip with her husband Barry to Los Angeles and the joys of baking cakes, bread and pies.

Ben's birthday finally arrived and Ben, Hannah, Graham, Ben's school friend Nikos and his squash partner Lucy all turned up at Silver Hatch in Graham's Audi RS6. Ben went through the compulsory introductory briefing, he put on the racing outfit and helmet and went over to Hannah, Graham, Nikos and Lucy and shouted "look good don't I, I'm gonna be the next Schumacher!"

He got into the racing car and started the engine; it was a modified formula one racing car with the speed limited to one hundred and fifty miles an hour. Ben pressed on the accelerator, the engine first purred then growled, the car oozed power. Ben sped off for his first lap, his friends looked on and cheered as Ben drove past. As Ben completed the second lap Nikos shouted "he really likes racing, I reckon he should have taken it up as a career!" "Nothing is impossible" replied Graham ecstatically.

As time went on, Ben's friends wondered where he was. It had been almost twenty minutes and he still had not passed the start-finish line. Suddenly, there was the sound of sirens wailing in the distance. "What is that?" asked Graham pointing to the far side of the race track. "Looks like fire engines" replied Hannah.

After ten more minutes, they saw an ambulance racing down the track going towards where the fire engine was. "Someone must have been injured" guessed Lucy, "yeah I only hope it is not serious" said Nikos worryingly. The friends then looked at each other in silence before Graham blurted out "I hope Ben is not involved." "I think we should ask someone at reception" said Hannah, Graham nodded and got up, "I'll go and ask" he said feverishly before turning and walking away.

Graham returned ten minutes later slouched and with a sullen look on his face. Hannah saw him in the distance and ran towards him "what is it, where is Ben, is he okay?" Graham paused and looked at her tearfully. Hannah yelled "answer me, is he okay?" Graham spoke meekly "I'm afraid he lost control of the car, they are going to take him to the Royal Infirmary. We better go, it doesn't look good though." "Oh my god" exclaimed Hannah, "I can't believe it."

As the group made their way to Graham's car Hannah turned to Graham "I should tell Lisa, she will want to know." Graham nodded in agreement "did Ben tell you about his secret present for Lisa?" asked Graham dolefully, "no he didn't, what special present?" enquired Hannah inquisitively. "He knew he messed up on their first date, so he sent her flowers and a card yesterday with tickets for both of them to Paris on the Eurostar for next weekend." Hannah gulped and stood still for a few moments in amazement.

Hannah pressed speed dial three on her mobile phone, Lisa answered the call and said excitedly "Hi Hannah, you won't believe what I've just received. Ben sent me the most beautiful flowers I've ever seen as well as tickets for us to Paris next weekend for our second date." Hannah was silent. "Hannah are you there?" bellowed Lisa. "Lisa I need to tell you something" said Hannah softly. "What is it, is something wrong?" exclaimed Lisa.

"Ben has been injured, we don't know how seriously yet, we are about to go to the hospital." "What do you mean injured?"

asked Lisa. "Graham bought him a racing experience for his birthday at Silver Hatch and" said Hannah before Lisa angrily interrupted "What racing experience, you never told me, you just said it was a trip to Silver Hatch. Ben should not go racing, the fortune cookie at the Chinese restaurant said so. You remember?" "What fortune cookie?" asked Hannah mystified. "Ben's fortune cookie message at Shanghai Express stated that danger would arise if he were to go racing" said Lisa irate. "Why didn't you tell me?" cried Hannah before Graham yelled "Hannah let's go."

Hannah spoke frantically on her phone as she rushed towards Graham's car "I gotta go, we're going directly to the hospital. I will call you when I'm there, are you sure that message in the fortune cookie said that Ben should not go racing?" "I remember it as clear as day, it said that danger lay in the fast lane. Call me as soon as you get there" replied Lisa anxiously.

Ben's friends arrived half an hour later at the hospital, they immediately asked the receptionist where Ben was. "He is in intensive care, you need to speak to surgeon Mc Farley, he'll be able to help you," replied the receptionist. They all rushed to the intensive care unit, they could see a lot of commotion on one side of the unit. Graham called out to the nearest doctor "I'm looking for Ben Wickes, I understand he has been brought here?" The doctor nodded and uttered "one moment please" before trotting off in the opposite direction.

After what seemed like an eternity, the doctor returned accompanied by another doctor who had a grim look on his face. The second doctor didn't make eye contact with any of the group until he introduced himself as Mr. Mc Farley. In a soft tone and with his head swaying from side to side Mc Farley explained in an almost academic fashion "Ben suffered severe internal injuries, he had several fractured ribs and a fractured skull. He suffered major head trauma from the crash and unfortunately there was nothing we could do to save him. He died ten minutes ago, I am very very sorry, my heartfelt condolences." He then turned to the other doctor and whispered in his ear before proceeding to walk off in a timely fashion.

The other doctor spoke hesitantly "Mr. Mc Farley had to rush off since he is treating a critically ill patient, if there is anything I can do to assist please let me know. Ben is in booth eight down the corridor to your right." Hannah burst out crying as she fell to her knees. Lucy hugged her and tried to console her but she continued to sob loudly. Graham and Nikos stood silently in shock, they both felt like they had just been hit by a freight train travelling at over a hundred miles an hour.

Lucy grabbed Hannah and helped her to her feet. Hannah wiped the tears from her face before taking out her phone and dialling Lisa's number. Lisa answered on the first ring "Any news?" she exclaimed. "Oh my god Lisa" said Hannah mournfully "that fortune cookie was right, Ben should never have gone racing. Ben died ten minutes ago in intensive care, I'm so sorry honey."

A Bus Journey

2010.

A London bus stop.

Early June and pleasantly warm.

Around 11am in the morning.

The following are at the bus stop:

WIZARD, (Phillip), a fifty-five year old civil servant

AGNES, a retired septuagenarian

ROBERT, a seventeen year old school boy

TIMMY, a scrawly twenty-something heroin addict

ACT ONE – AT THE BUS STOP

WIZARD

Morning Agnes, off to the shops again?

AGNES

Yes Phillip, I need some more groceries and going to the shops gives me a reason to get out of the house

(Pauses and looks up)

Isn't it such a sunny day?

WIZARD

I've seen better for June but I guess it's not that bad

(A car speeds past)

Look at that car, it is ridiculous the speed at which they drive
nowadays

AGNES

(Looks and nods)

WIZARD

I read in the local Guardian last week that a young lad was killed
when a motorist ran him down at a zebra crossing in Croydon,
turned out the driver was drunk. What a waste of life, I mean..

AGNES

I feel sorry for the family

WIZARD

I think they are too soft today, they should bring back national
service, give the youth some discipline

AGNES

A good idea but I don't think that will happen

WIZARD

Just last Saturday a sixteen year old girl was stabbed in the High Street

(AGNES gasps)

WIZARD

Seems she got into an argument with another group of girls

AGNES

I never go to the High Street at night; my neighbour Mavis tells me that there is always trouble there on evenings. The police are always being called out and..

WIZARD

It's alcohol as well. Too much alcohol and the fists go flying

AGNES

I think we need some more police on the street

WIZARD

Yes regular coppers not these new coppers, these pcso's who cannot arrest or physically restrain someone even if they suspect them of committing a crime. I think it's just policing on the cheap. Why can't they just have more regular coppers?

AGNES

I like seeing them on the street, makes you feel more secure

WIZARD

I see them now and then but I think it's policing on the cheap

(Breathes deeply and shuffles on the spot)

The kids of today need discipline and hard work. Let them spend two years in the army, that'll teach em. My army days were the best days of my life

(AGNES stands up)

WIZARD

Are you all right Agnes?

AGNES

Ah yes, my joints aren't what they used to be

WIZARD

The bus should be here in five minutes if the indicator is correct, which it usually is

AGNES

Good. At least I don't have to wait twenty minutes like I did yesterday!

(ROBERT comes to the bus stop playing music on his mobile phone and spits out chewing gum on the street)

(Uneasy tension)

WIZARD

Can you turn that music down a little young man?

(ROBERT pretends he didn't hear WIZARD. He continues to listen to the music while doing a little bop to the beat)

WIZARD

(Speaks a little louder)

Can you turn that music down a little?

ROBERT

(Annoyed by WIZARD'S request)

What's wrong gramps, it ain't loud at all, need to turn down that hearing aid a little

WIZARD

Look, I've asked you nicely to turn down that music of yours or I will report you to your school

(AGNES sits back down)

ROBERT

Take it easy gramps, I'll switch it off.

(Switches off music and puts phone into his jacket pocket)

(Looks at WIZARD and laughingly retorts)

Aren't you the bloke who is always walking round the streets dropping stuff in people's letterboxes?

WIZARD

I am a member of neighbourhood watch and do some work for a few local charities so you may have seen me here and there

ROBERT

You been waiting long for the bus?

WIZARD

It should be here in a couple of minutes

ROBERT

(Loud guffaws, points to a man walking towards them on the opposite side of the road and exclaims)

Oh look there's Timmy, the crazy homeless guy who walks around all day asking people for money. He smells like shit. The guy is a proper psycho

(TIMMY continues walking along the pavement, he looks up and sees the trio at the bus stop opposite looking at him. He crosses over the road jauntily)

(ROBERT turns his head to the right to avoid eye contact with TIMMY)

TIMMY

(To ROBERT)

Yo bruv, can u spare us some change?

ROBERT

Nah mate, ain't got none

TIMMY

Can you spare us fifty pence, I need to get some grub

ROBERT

Sorry mate

WIZARD

(Walks towards TIMMY)

Here is two pounds

TIMMY

(Bows to WIZARD gratefully)

Thanks bruv, you saved me life

(AGNES gasps and holds her breath as the stench from TIMMY reaches her nostrils)

(TIMMY turns and walks on jadedly)

ROBERT

(Turning to WIZARD)

You shouldn't have given it to him, he'll only use it to buy drugs

WIZARD

(Turns and looks at TIMMY)

What a waste, he's probably on heroin, he looks so gaunt and seems like he's in a daze

AGNES

(Gets up and moves slowly towards the road)

At last the bus

(All three get on the bus. ROBERT first, then AGNES followed by WIZARD)

ACT TWO - ON THE BUS

CHRISTIAN and JULIUS, two twenty something NEETS (not in employment, education or training), both became best friends during their stay at a young offenders' institution

ROGER, a family man in his forties

BUS DRIVER, a man in his late thirties

OFFICER 1, a police constable in his forties

OFFICER 2, a police constable in her twenties

CHRISTIAN and JULIUS are already on the bus, sitting together at the back of the upper deck, ROGER is sitting at the front of the upper deck.

ROBERT sits towards the back of the upper deck. WIZARD and AGNES sit on the lower deck.

ROBERT listens to music on his mobile phone, this time using headphones.

JULIUS

(Turns to CHRISTIAN)

Yo, check da school boy wiv his mobe, looks like pay time

CHRISTIAN

(Nods and grins. He walks along the upper deck and sits next to ROBERT, blocking his exit)

Yo mate, giv us ur phone, I need to make a call

ROBERT

(Pulls his headphones from his ear to hear what was said)

What did you say?

CHRISTIAN

I said I need to borrow ya phone, cos I need to make a call

ROBERT

Sorry mate, ain't got no credit on it

JULIUS

(JULIUS sits on the window seat behind ROBERT. He grabs ROBERT by the neck)

Listen to da man, give us ur phone and ya money or I'll cut ya with a blade

(ROBERT freezes with fear)

CHRISTIAN

(Puts his hand into ROBERT's jacket pocket, takes out his mobile phone and puts it into a pocket in his cargo pants)

Where's ya money?

ROBERT

(Says sheepishly)

Ain't got none

JULIUS

(Whispers into ROBERT's ear)

Don't lie to da man or I'll kill ya

CHRISTIAN

(Puts his hand into ROBERT's right trousers pocket and pulls out his wallet, he puts this into another pocket in his cargo pants)

What u got in ya left pocket?

ROBERT

(Shakes his head from side to side)

Just my oyster card

JULIUS

Give it to da man and I'll let ya go

ROBERT

(Takes out his oyster card and gives it to CHRISTIAN. CHRISTIAN puts it into the same pocket in his cargo pants as ROBERT's wallet)

JULIUS

Don't tell no-one and you'll be safe cos I don't wanna have to come back for u, we're tha ghosts of tha undaground..

(JULIUS gets up and goes to press the bell so the bus stops at the next bus stop. CHRISTIAN follows him close behind. They make their way down the stairs)

ROBERT

(ROBERT sits frozen for five minutes. He then approaches ROGER)

I've just been mugged by those two, those two..

ROGER

Which two?

ROBERT

Those two guys who were sitting at the back, one with the puffer jacket and the other with the white baseball cap and baggy cargo pants

ROGER

Really! I didn't see anything, I was reading the paper

(ROBERT sits down on the seat behind ROGER, resting his head on the rail at the back of ROGER's seat)

ROGER

Sorry mate have to get off the next stop, you better report it to the police

(ROGER gets up and goes down the stairs)

(ROBERT's bus stop comes and he goes downstairs, AGNES has got off but WIZARD is still on. WIZARD looks at ROBERT. ROBERT walks towards WIZARD)

Did you see those two guys who got off earlier, one with the puffer jacket and the other with the white baseball cap and baggy cargo pants?

WIZARD

Yes why?

ROBERT

They mugged me, they took my phone, my money and my oyster card. They threatened to stab me, I think one of them was carrying a knife

(ROBERT collapses into the seat in front of WIZARD)

WIZARD

Hold on lad, I'll be back in a tick

(WIZARD goes to the BUS DRIVER and tells him what has transpired. The BUS DRIVER stops the bus and asks all passengers to evacuate the bus)

(WIZARD returns to ROBERT to find him sitting up now)

WIZARD

The driver has radioed for the police and an ambulance. They should be here shortly

(ROBERT rests his head on the railing of the seat in front as WIZARD sits down opposite ROBERT)

WIZARD

Are you hurt?

ROBERT

Not really, one of them grabbed me by the neck and the other one took all my stuff

WIZARD

Thank god you were not seriously hurt, it could have turned out much worse

ROBERT

I still can't believe it, this has never happened to me before

WIZARD

Don't worry lad, those scum bags will get what they deserve

ROBERT

But those assholes, I can't let them get away with it

WIZARD

Leave that to the police, it's their job, the last thing we need is you going around with a group of your friends looking to get even

BUS DRIVER

Are you okay young man?

ROBERT

(Nods)

BUS DRIVER

The police and ambulance will be here shortly

ROBERT

(Nods)

(Police sirens wail)

OFFICER 1

(OFFICER 1 walks towards the bus. WIZARD approaches him)

WIZARD

Apparently the lad on the bus has been mugged by two other lads, they roughed him up and took his valuables but he is not seriously hurt

OFFICER 1

Did you see the incident sir?

WIZARD

No, I was sitting downstairs at the time

OFFICER 1

Can you wait here one moment sir, my colleague will speak to you

WIZARD

Yes of course

OFFICER 1

(Walks onto the bus and speaks to ROBERT)

I heard you were mugged mate, are you hurt at all?

ROBERT

No I'm okay, they grabbed me and took my wallet, my mobile and my oyster card

OFFICER 1

(Takes out pad and pen and begins to write)

Can I take your name , address and telephone number?

ROBERT

Robert Preston, 45 Addiscombe Parkway, Sutton SM1 7TY. My home number is 02086441399. The number of the mobile phone that was stolen is 07967189805.

OFFICER 1

And what is your date of birth Robert?

ROBERT

11ᵗʰ of May 1993

OFFICER 1

Can you explain to me what happened?

ROBERT

Yes I was sitting upstairs and was approached by these two guys, one had a white baseball cap and baggy cargo pants and the other one had a puffer jacket. The one with the baseball cap sat next to me and asked to use my phone. When I told him it had no credit the other guy grabbed me by the neck and threatened to stab me unless I hand over my phone. The guy in the cap then took my phone and asked for my money. When I told him I didn't have any the other guy threatened to kill me. Then the guy with the cap checked my pockets and took my wallet and my oyster card

OFFICER 1

Can you describe exactly what they looked like and what they were wearing?

ROBERT

The one with the baseball cap was white, around 6′ 2″, I reckon around twenty five. The baseball cap had a Nike logo on it, he was also wearing black baggy cargo pants, a Nike sweater and white trainers but I can't remember what make. The other guy I didn't see too well. He was mixed race, around 5′ 9″, I reckon a bit older than the other one

OFFICER 1

Can you remember what the mixed race guy was wearing?

ROBERT

He was wearing blue jeans and a black puffer jacket. I can't remember anything else

OFFICER 1

Do you remember any scars, tattoos, gold teeth or other marks that may distinguish them?

ROBERT

The one with the baseball cap had a gold ring on his right hand and had something wrong with some of his teeth. I mean they were all crooked and a few at the back were missing. It looked like he never brushed them. I don't remember much about the other guy but he did have very short afro hair.

OFFICER 1

Do you remember if they spoke with an accent?

ROBERT

Just London accents although the guy in the baseball cap had an east London accent

OFFICER 1

How about the guy in the puffer jacket?

ROBERT

A south London accent

OFFICER 1

Can you remember where they got off?

ROBERT

At Parsons Corner I think

(Chatter on OFFICER 1's radio)

(Ambulance siren wails)

OFFICER 1

Come with me Robert, we'll get you checked out with the paramedics

ROBERT

I'm all right

OFFICER 1

It will only take a minute

(ROBERT gets up to leave the bus accompanied by OFFICER 1)

(Meanwhile outside the bus OFFICER 2 has been speaking with WIZARD)

OFFICER 2

(To WIZARD)

Sir, can I take your name, address and telephone number?

WIZARD

Yes, my name is Phillip Artingham, I live at 23 Bromsgrove Terrace, Wimbledon, London SW20 3HU. My home telephone number is 02087678233.

OFFICER 2

Sir, can you please describe the suspects as best you can?

WIZARD

I didn't see them clearly. I do remember one was wearing a white baseball cap and had white sports shoes. He was the taller of the two, around 6' 1". The other wore a black jacket, he was a coloured chap, about 5' 7"

OFFICER 2

Was the one in the white baseball cap Caucasian?

WIZARD

Yes

OFFICER 2

Do you remember if any of them had any distinguishing or unusual features, like an unusually colourful jacket, any stains or marks, or were carrying any bags?

WIZARD

No I'm sorry, I only saw them leave the bus and didn't really look at them too closely

OFFICER 2

Thank you sir for your help, we may be in touch if we require any further information

WIZARD

Will be glad to assist

(WIZARD sees ROBERT leaving the bus walking towards the ambulance accompanied by OFFICER 1. He walks towards ROBERT)

WIZARD

Take care young man

ROBERT

Thank you

PART TWO

Acting

Ahoy there sailor! Riding the high seas of acting

Looking for an island to set down and set up camp

Long have I sailed earnestly looking for that refuge

Long shall I sail until I reach my journeys end

Ahead an iceburg! Abandon ship the captain shouts!

Many an actor has given up, exhausted from all the trials and tribulations

But I solider on like a bull on the rampage

Refusing to give in until my body breaks down and my bones crumble

I see the mirage! The bright lights and my name on Broadway!

I have high hopes and I want to push myself beyond all limits

Far and wide and high and low the acting fraternity trundles

Illuminating, entertaining and captivating the audience

Adapt or Die

The climate changes, adapt or die

No more fish in the sea, adapt or die

Lost your job, can't pay the mortgage, adapt or die

Can't read or write and have no patience, adapt or die

Addicted to gambling, women, drugs and alcohol, adapt or die

Your partner and friends leaves you, your parents and relatives die, you're on your own,

adapt or die

A-D-A-P-T

O-R

D-I-E

Agony, pain and ecstasy

Football is my religion

I feel the highs and lows

My spirit surges when my team goes ahead

And I close my eyes and pray when my team goes behind

I wear my replica shirt loud and proud

Since a lad of six I've supported my team through thick and thin

We've conquered Europe and been on top of the world

We've felt the joys of victory and I've celebrated through the night

I've been there when they've fallen and I've sung and shouted in support

I've been there in the great comebacks, those moments of sheer delight

Each toss and turn, each swerve and header, leaves me screaming and jumping around

Nothing can beat those sweet moments

Of agony, pain and ecstasy

Airport

I'm packed and all ready to go
To warm and tropical climes

You welcome me with open arms
You are the gateway to the world

Waiting patiently for gate call
I look at all the people in the hall

They're from all corners of the world
A shifting kaleidoscope of humanity

AK-47

I look at you   You look
                                                     away

Is it because of my beard and AK-47?   Probably so

I ask you to speak and tell me who sent you   You do not
say

I tell you a story of fairies and daffodils
that my grandfather once told me   You do not
                                                     listen

I try to befriend you and tell you my
life story   You are not
                                                     interested

We're both the same age, love football,
girls and music   You seem
                                                     unconvinced

I explain that you could be just like me,
if you were born in similar circumstances   You disagree

At last some dialogue, I ask you to explain   You explain

I say that people are the same irrespective

of country, creed or race

You agree

I ask you why we need to fight, I ask you if
we could instead lay down our arms and
dance?

You say our
countries are
at

war and that
you   have
orders   from
your
superiors

I ask you if we can sit down and have coffee
when the war is finally over

You smile

[The commander comes in and shouts]

You look
fearful

I explain that I have been ordered to take
you to A-block

You say
orders are
orders

I wish you good luck and escort you to
A-block

You thank
me for our
brief

tête-à-tête

I reach out to shake your hand   [we shake
                                                   hands]

Alaska

The spectacular mountain vistas

The vast untouched wilderness

The beautiful snow capped peaks

The sheer power of nature

The magnificent lakes

Aleatory

The sacred covenant between man and creator

Beyond quantum mechanics and Newtonian physics

No man can be an island even if he believes hell is other people

The Dharma wheel keeps turning and the bell continues to toll

Walking the eightfold path in the falling rain

Notwithstanding any excruciating pain or impulsive carnal
compulsions

Listening intently to the Yi as the Qi force surges

Streams of consciousness melting into the cosmic river

Unbalanced thoughts still trying to upset the equilibrium

Only love opens the gates of the soul

Alien one and two

From afar emerged aliens one and two

Looking for what was never theirs and trying to capture that which cannot be captured

When you seek counsel from two hundred friends

You get two hundred contradictory responses

When you listen to your heart it will always be true

So long as you have the faith, patience and persistence to listen carefully

No more aliens treading in pastures that bear the no-entry sign

No more all night telephone lectures on Nicomachean Ethics

Then right living, peace and harmony

Will reign over the poets and philosopher kings

Alpha and Omega

Every beginning must have an end
Nature will map out its own course
Try as we may to defy Mother Nature
It always has the upper hand
Since Mother Nature is the omnipresent
The Alpha and Omega

Amma

She tirelessly works for good, for the sick, needy and poor

And all her family and friends appreciate her devotion and her love

Radiating positive energy, giving constant encouragement, blessings and more

Overseas and overland, her love spreads across the globe like a migrating dove

Journeying from Guyana, until she landed on England's fair shores

Indian Madonna, performing bhakti and dispersing shakti from above

Never ceasing to amaze, her name will be part of Yorkshire folklore

In honour of Amma, this poem filled with love

Ancient Egypt

From a distance the pyramids at Giza look spectacular and as you get closer to them they began to look very majestic, you began to feel a sense of what it was like to live in the time of the Pharaohs, with all the pomp, ceremony and lavish banquets that they had.

That was a time of discovery, of exploring the unknown and pushing the boundaries of the possible, of taking building and construction to new heights of development, of embracing a whole new culture rich with history and adventure.

It must have been fascinating to walk through the Valley of the Kings and feel the sense of grandeur they had. A sense of exploring not only the world and the surrounding area, but also oneself and the power and potential of the inner self to be creative and imaginative enough to invent the elementary foundations of modern maths, and to develop the structure of modern language through the use of cuneiform and elaborate & sophisticated pictographs and hieroglyphics.

Taking a cruise down the Nile from Cairo to Luxor is an unforgettable experience, not least because the food served en route and at stop-overs is a taste sensation, full of spices and new stimulating aromas that left the palette invigorated. The cruise was like a voyage of discovery, travelling from the more built up and heavily populated capital city down towards the more open, sparsely populated south. The scenery changed from being lush green to more savannah yellow-brown. The cruise was so gentle that you felt you were almost not moving, just floating and drifting smoothly along as you looked out on the vast plains that at one time in the past were the very foundation of civilisation, one the founding centres of human development. Being able to connect with such history is a truly fascinating and fulfilling experience.

Arcadian

Long lost are the days of antiquity

Where the Mycenaean's flourished in the Peloponnese

They were always at home in love's equinox, the pastoral utopia of Homer

Until the waning Moon triggered the Bronze Age retreat

At the beginning of the new millennium

Space flight, nuclear power and technological delight

Unintentionally spawn digital overload, over-stimulated and flummoxed craniums

Until C_2H_5OH comes to the rescue and everyone elopes to distant lands in order to sing besides campfires whilst dancing in the starlight

As the twilight of the noughties fade and the twenty-tens midsummer's eve draws closer

The rays of a new golden age cascade past the Gherkin's lintel and the London Eye's pods

A renaissance of Ovid grips the eager denizens of the boroughs

The Novus ordo seclorum votive to placate the omnipresent gods

Awareness

Acute awareness of the human condition

Brings new awareness of the need for meditation

Calm and unattached awareness of the metaphysical dilemma

Dawn of a new era and time to chant the new age mantra

Engaged in critical reasoning to actively engage the
philosophical spectrum

Fill the existential angst with succour and sing melodramatic
anthems

Go further into oneself than one has ever been before

Harangue the haughty dullard secreting mendacious verbal
spores

Ingratiate with the erudite scholars locked in their ivory tower

Just as charlatans and sceptics traduce the many, they are
painfully aware that truth alone is power

Knaves and petulant scoundrels seek to lock everyone into the
accumulation consumerist sideshow

Listless and pathetic, the sleeping majority trudge along in
blissful unawareness living life in the shadows

Megalomania, Kleptomania, Pyromania, Monomania,
Hypomania will only leave one fallow

Non judgmental awareness is all one needs to grow

Organic growth through selfless awareness and enlightenment
will dawn

Powerful divine lodestar guides believers who are drawn

Quiet sublimation through the chakras brings enchantment and
delight

Resplendent waves of consciousness rise until the spirit finally sees the light

Suddenly instant attraction occurs and sensory overload interposes

Thrust into the higher realms of awareness the body elevates and the soul glows

Until nirvana is reached and there is a union of body, mind and soul

Verity must prevail and consciousness can become an integrated whole

Worldwide harmony through individual awareness and collective spiritual union

Xoanon and demiurge, many religions, many creeds, but emanating from the

same scion

Yearning for a better tomorrow, requires us to work hard today

Zorba the Buddha is one path towards the union of matter and soul, each new day offering opportunities to take the enlightened new way, a new way of becoming as we enter a new century and a new millennium

A brother from another mother

Greco Buddhist philosophical musings with diamond white political chatter,

Brothers in arms, in the good times and the bad,

Constructive criticisms are exhorted as they play devil's advocate, both consciously trying to get to the heart of the matter,

Never a dull moment, because life is never dull, imbibing a daily melodramatic cocktail of transient happy moments mixed with the sad.

One a Jedi master, the other was an apprentice; now the learned apprentice is heralded as the supreme master,

As the unknown future inexorably rolls towards the brothers from another mother,

And incessant gyrations of the gyre leaves them more tasks in the "to do" in-tray, time inevitably seems to tick by so much faster,

Yet onwards they march, heads held high like marines, heavy backpacks in tow, on life's precious journey, together as brothers.

A brown leaf

I stood there in awe, in silence, appreciating, taking in with all my senses.

All the time I go through life at over a hundred miles an hour.

I never really get a chance to appreciate nature and its beauty.

Standing on a Himalayan mountain peak surveying the wild untouched
wilderness made me breathe a little deeper.

As I began to take in the sights, sounds and smells, I melted into a leaf and floated to the ground.

A coffee interlude

A place to meet and browse the web
Or read the latest fiction bestseller and glace at the newspaper
Or a place to take a break from a hectic day
And indulge in a special caffeine treat

Starbucks, Café Nero, Coffee Café Day, Costa or my local
I've enjoyed coffee in coffee shops across the world
A different fragrance, a different nomenclature
But the same universal love of the coffee interlude

Why do I love the whole coffee experience?
Is it the coffee or is it the coffee shop's ambience?
Why do I feel strange when I miss my daily caffeine drink?
Is it because I'm addicted to the coffee interlude?

A different time, a different place...

I would be a king or perhaps a servant

We would be lovers or perhaps friends

I'd sing for a living or perhaps play football professionally

I'd have lots of brothers and sisters or perhaps be an orphan

I'd be a millionaire or perhaps homeless

I'd be a film star or perhaps a star gazer

The grass is always greener...perhaps.

A familiar journey

We've travelled this way a hundred times

Early mornings and early evenings

We've sat on different carriages on different tube trains

We've read different papers and listened to different songs

We are all passing faces on passing subway trains

Temporary adornments in the diurnal kaleidoscope that feeds the visual appetite

A constant stream of images disregarded and removed to the mind's recycle bin

Forgotten about once we reach work in the morning or home in the evening

I sit across from you and you look back at me

Do you think I exist and do I think you exist?

Or does our mind switch off and we all become robots

Until we reach the end of our journey and we become human again

A follicular challenge

Twenty one
Is much too young
To have a follicular challenge

Hair falling out
One by one
A daily battle ensues to save each one

Hair grafts
Lotions
5a reductase

Trying to keep baldness at bay
And the ego sated
Hoping to emerge with confidence intact

Even prodigious Harley Street trichologists pontificate
Unable to agree
Instead expatiate prodigally

Once the crowning glory
Now a forlorn love story
About a topic that is now thorny

Last resorts for the needy

Are alchemy and black magic

Leading to a result that will only be tragic

A game of dice

God doesn't play dice
Or so Einstein thought

Life is a game of dice; throw caution to the wind
Better live life like Yudhisthira than hide in the shadows

You try to play the odds until you realize it is vision and belief
that really matter
Only when you push your boundaries will you expand your
horizons

A great movie

I love poetry that is captivating and grabs my attention. I would be reading a poem and be so engrossed that I focus on the words and they would almost come to life. A great poem is like a great movie, you enter the theatre hall full of anticipation, awaiting a two hour adventure, surrendering to the whole movie experience and eager for excitement and exhilaration. The movie always has a structure, starting off slowly and then building up gradually to a compelling climax. The best movies are the ones that you reflect on for a long time afterwards and they are the ones that leave you feeling fulfilled and fascinated.

A Job

Good salary, £12,000 per annum with the possibility of earning up to £20,000 from overtime.

Double overtime outside contracted hours (*but you won't get it*)

Mandatory rest and lunch breaks (*but only if you insist and if you do, we will replace you*)

Friendly and supportive work environment (*if you tow the line and don't speak too much*)

Good health and pension scheme (*not by us but provided by the state*)

Job security (*or so you think*)

Work for a company that values talented, articulate individuals with a good eye for detail, good numeric and IT skills and excellent interpersonal skills (*but we prefer robots and people who are like door mats, so we can walk all over them*)

Recruiting now.

A new flat world

Once the world was flat or so we thought

Then the world was round or so we were taught

Globalization, mass migration, the weightless economy and technological innovations

Friedman's thesis, an imaginative leitmotiv

A new planet

What if we both left this fair world of ours

And travelled across the universe in a yellow submarine

Until we settled on a new planet

Just like Earth but without human inhabitants

We would be the new Adam and Eve

The founders of a new race of new planetarians

We would spread love, joy, wisdom and peace

Then pass the baton to our progeny and hope they spread even more love than we managed to

A pigeon flew over the nest

My dear faithful companion
Ever eager, curious and alert
From country barn to penthouse suite
You grace us with your presence

Oh sentient friend, the greatest savant
Tell me your story, for you see so much
The farmer ploughing his fields by day
The policeman patrolling the street by night

You're there when the Sun is rising
You're there when the stars twinkle bright
You've seen the storm in the horizon
You've seen the quilt of snow down below

How wild and free you seem to be
How your spirit roams serenely
How you glide magnificently in the sky
From chimney to chimney across the city

Buffeted away from Trafalgar Square
Your company Lord Nelson doth dearly miss
When all is said and done, you'll not be undone
You'll be watching from atop once again

A psychic episode

If I picture something, can you guess what it may be?
Just stop, relax, close your eyes and let your imagination go

Put your hands in mine because it creates a stronger connection
Still no luck, then let me describe a little

We're both together; you're having a great time and feeling
really good
Can you imagine that?

We're on a tropical island paradise
Just you and me

We've just been exploring the island together
Relaxing in the sun and swimming in the crystal clear blue sea

We go into the beach hut and munch on fresh tasty food
Then we sit together on the beach looking up and watching the
stars

I hold your hand and tell you how beautiful you are
How you make my heart race and how you make my soul soar
as if it is dancing in a celestial rhapsody with the Moon and stars

We chat and laugh and then chat some more
Until I hold you close and kiss you gently

A sign of the times

In a twenty-four hour international world I need twenty-four hour news

The net at my fingertips and access to the latest information wherever I am

The ipod, the iphone and the next big app to keep me prepped

When time is short and I've no time for dating one person at a time

I try speed dating instead

And for keyboard jockeys, there's Second Life

It's a whole new way of life

It's a sign of the times

Planes going into buildings and bombs on the tube

Technological savvy terrorist organisations with PhD recruits

Now there are terrorist states with renegade nukes, it's enough to leave me spooked

Full spectrum warfare will leave no stone unturned

Forget the raison d'être

It's a game of cat and mouse

It's a whole new way of life

It's a sign of the times

States have their borders but borders melt away

When El Nino, volcanic ash and tsunami's strike

A collective response is the only way

As the polar caps recede

And deforestation continues apace

The fragile eco system hangs precariously in the balance

It's a whole new way of life

It's a sign of the times

A theory of justice

Justice is in the eye of the beholder, it is subjective and mutable, said Caesar

Justice is universal, it is for now and forever, objective and principled, said the senator

But if we were in the original position behind the veil of ignorance, we'd have justice as fairness, said Rawls

Au contraire mon amie, justice is a matter of entitlements, screamed Nozick

But what of traditions and the community, shouted the communitarians

And what about the gambler, added Dworkin

"All in good time" replied the sleep deprived exam weary jurisprudence student, "I'm still reading Socrates."

Bacchus

From the Californian vineyards
To the Chelsea Wharf courtyards
Let the vines grow sturdily and rapidly
Let the wine flow freely

The intoxication of life
Ebullient revelry casting away a bereft and insalubrious life
Eclipsed by the rainbow of inebriation
Singing, dancing, performing a skittish Sun salutation

Don Quixote's windmills come alive after too much moonshine
The grapes of past poets now maturing into the finest wine
Raising a wine glass to the ceiling
For at last the wine has summoned the primeval feeling

Becoming fully aware...

Your first kiss

When you won a prize at school

When you came top of your class at university

On the day you get married

At the birth of your first child

When you are falling in love

When you score the winning goal

When you are riding a rollercoaster

When you pilot a plane

When you are skydiving

Beyond existence

Beyond the known lies the unknown

The knower knows, the theorist theorises, the seer sees and the doer does

Beyond Sartre, Camus, Kierkegaard and Wittgenstein

Is an essence that transcends language, culture and philosophy

Beyond deconstruction, the Simulacrum and the postmodern fable

Lies a reality that is unchanged since time immemorial

Big Brother

An Endemol adventure

Twas quite a deal

Promising fame and fortune from reality television

Some series were good and some were not

Yet voyeurs we all were

At last the end is nigh and big brother waves goodbye

Blah!

He said "blah", she said "blah, blah"
I said "no blah, its blah blah and blah"

She replies "don't you blah, blah blah"
I said "why not, it's blah blah blah"

He extorted "is blah poetry, or a load of blah?"
She concluded "blah is blah, it's full of blah"

"No, blah is just a load of blah" I solemnly confessed
"The blah is out there" so blah blah blah!

Botox

Skin deep is the depth of my soul

I need to get the next fix of ambrosia and nectar

Eternal youth is my only cure

The elixir of youth the only thing I crave

Fighting grey hair, obesity and wrinkles, fighting the aging
process and fighting nature

My portrait to be frozen, timeless like Peter Pan

A poison is now my saviour

Injected here and there with a little pain and some costly labour

Just another confectionery, a pick me up off the shelf beverage,
off the shelf, in a plethora of flavours

Young forever and forever young.

Bruce Lee

Saturday night, alone I sit
The rain hits the window for more than just a bit

"What's on the telly?" My mind asks
Nothing as usual, my evening is empty

Alone it sits, gathering dust with fingerprints all over it
I pick it up and look at the cover

Oh memories
It's like a welcoming mother

I put the DVD into the player and relax on the sofa
The titles start to role but I can't wait for Bruce

Enter the Dragon
Has once again entered my imagination

Bucket list

A list most people have not heard about

A list most people never even think about

A list most people never write

The bucket list

A list of things one wants to do before one dies

Life's twenty first century shopping list

Bucolic

Can there be any better life than living in the country at one with nature?

Free from the big smoke
And the Congestion Charge's cloak

Where the spirit can roam free
Overflowing with glee

Buddha

Even happiness is dukkha
All that is born will eventually die

Prajna, Sila and Samadhi
The archetypal triad of truth

When bodhi is attained
The self will be extinguished

Through surrender and release
Everyone can be free to see the nature of the One

The circle of life will one day be complete
The soul energy will pass, its energy transforming but never dissipating

Living in a world of samsara
Nothing stays the same

Total immersion in the river of life
Each drop, one life

One cosmic being, one truth

Buridan's Ass

Each moment presents a thousand possibilities
A thousand stars calling from the heavens

The infinite sky with infinite possibilities
Offering the Moon and the stars to the bravest souls

Hitting and missing
Striking chords and melodies

A constant battle between Los and Urizen
Trying to escape the gravitational pull of an event horizon

The scales of utilitarianism trying to balance again
Until instinct and intuition drive the body forward once more

Unending Dasein, Being and Time
Another paradox to deliberate over at bedtime

Camels in the desert

Camels in the desert slowing traversing the dunes

No path in front and the path already trodden now covered by sand

Just like those camels we humans are travellers in the desert

The sands of time will slowly wash away all trace of the path we have walked

Ambling along with magnificence and beauty

The camels walk on with great conviction and purpose

Through the blistering heat at noon and the chilly desert night

Nothing can stop these great desert behemoths

From horizon to horizon the view remains the same

But carry on without riposte the camels they do

The desert transporters have immense patience and unyielding will

They can certainly teach us humans a thing or two

Cameron

Fresh face and fresh impetus
Fresh wisdom comes to old Westminster

New ideas and a new direction
A new way to make the nation proud again

Faced with the task of economic rejuvenation
And achieving a balanced budget

Compassionate Conservatism and inclusive democracy
A new way forward without the usual hypocrisy

Full of acumen, alacrity and perspicuity
Beguiling and brimming with bitumen
The gentle bulldog he is.

A cool charming charismatic exterior
And an erudite, thoughtful and contemplative interior
The gentle bulldog he is.

An eye for the future and an ear to the ground
Big changes and the Big Society on his mind
The gentle bulldog he is.

Carthage

260 BCE

Numidian and Berber assassins

And a retinue of war elephants

Fighting the Romans, Iberians and mercenaries

In the lush and golden lands of the Mediterranean basin

216 BCE

Carthage rising! Feel the force

Of Hannibal's finest armies

Robed in diamonds and pearls

Advancing in search of glory

140 BCE

Outpost of the empire

Crushed by Roman zeal

The velvet cover of the desert sand

Hiding the ruins of ancient Carthage

2010 CE

Ancient Carthage! We behold

In folksongs and folktales

An empire that rose above the mire

To shower the Romans with fire

CCTV

You see me here and you see me there
You know me better than my mom

You are the omnipresent guiding eye
The one I cannot hide from

Hide and seek I may have played
But you have seen it all in your days

Your archives must be an amazing compilation
Of life unfolding across the years

Initial furore you may have caused
An Orwellian vision to despair

But now your presence we don't care
Your ever growing reach goes unnoticed

The perpetual watcher, guardian and overseer
The ubiquitous innocuous CCTV camera

Central Park

A sanctuary from the downturn swirl
Tempting New Yorkers at all times of year

Presidents, joggers, dogs, boys and girls
You've seen them all throughout your years

Cessna 152

Flying like a bird across the Sussex valleys
I feels like the world is my playground

Nerves race at take off before calm is restored once cruising at altitude
I feel like a feather in the wind, so light, lithe and carefree

When turbulence strikes I feel like I am in a dingy on the high seas
I bank left then right before bringing the plane horizontal again

The Cessna soars in the sky as magnificently as an eagle
More majestic than the behemoth Boeing or Airbus carriers

Just like a bird up in the sky
I was born a man who now can fly

Chickens coming home to roost

You think it's a good idea, so you make the play

It turns out well; you capture the land, its people and its
resources

You reap the rewards but you reap what you sow

Glory and victory now may mean nowt to future generations

The post colonial entrails scattered across distant frontiers

Leaving cartographers salivating at the constant revisions

We create a mess that we leave for others to resolve

As unwelcome as Coetzee's Colonel Joll

You reached a new peak

You conquered the wilderness

Nature tamed, nature rebuked

Jungles dethroned, forests cauterised

Man's advances may be considered salutary progress to the
current generation

But may reap havoc on future generations as they rue the day

When the chickens we let loose today

Come home to roost tomorrow

Childhood Innocence

Experiencing each new day in a Peter Pan way
Happy, eager and free

Far from the mind are evil thoughts
That adults develop over the years

Life seems so enthralling and new
The concept of time has never come to mind

Just exploring and growing
Learning and laughing

Childhood swings

Always keeping a merry sound

Whenever I jumped onto the merry-go-round

Just thinking of my primary school playground

Brings back memories so profound

Jumping, skipping, playing hop scotch

As all the other children watch

Conker games and jumping jacks

Eating pancakes with maple syrup and scrumptious chocolate flapjacks

Parents pushing swings back and forth

Until the swings build up quite a force

So the children cling on with all their might

In case they slip and fly through the air like a kite

Chillaxin'

On the beach	out of reach
On the train	without refrain
On the plane	my ipad entertains
At home	it's just like Rome
At work	I boldly explore like
Captain Kirk	
Chill	axin'

Christmas Wish

When you look into my eyes
My temperature starts to rise

When you stand next to me
A sudden rush of energy runs right through me

My heart skips a beat
Each time you hug me when we greet

Mistletoe and wine
Can make Christmas feel sublime

But my one Christmas wish
The only thing that I wish

Is to feel your body next to mine
From dusk to when the first rays of sun break through the night
skyline

Only you can take me higher
And fuel the flames of desire

Like teenagers on a cold winter night kept warm by each others
body heat
Electricity flows right through me, your touch banishes the
winter cold into retreat

I am forever under your spell and await patiently for your rescue

When my Christmas wish comes true

Cialdini's Principles

Driven in whatever ye may do
Driven to be the best you can

Ignite the fire that lurks within
Ignite the passion and fuel the flame

Application not theorisation, through fearless persistence
Angels in heaven always guarding and protecting thee

No ego, no mind, let the spirit run free
Never retreat or surrender, there's no time for that

Go far from your safe harbour and spread the good news
Go into the wilderness and sow the mustard seed

Experience each moment as if it were your last
Experience life fully like a camel in the desert

Let go of all obstacles that are holding you back
Let love overflow and fill each second

Observe the cosmic dance played out all around you
Only one Sun, one Moon, one Earth and one YOU in the whole
universe

Class Introductions

TEACHER: okay Tony, your turn, please introduce yourself to the class

TONY: I'm Tony, and I'm twenty two

I like going out and I like to wine and dine
I like partying all night and I like girls who look fine
I like going on holiday and love places with lots of sunshine
I like travelling and meeting new people all the time
I like the latest clothes but don't like if they cost too many nickels and dimes
I like animals and going to zoos and all things feline

I can't wait till I'm rich and famous and I'm driving fancy cars
I can't wait till Global Gathering when it again will be partytime
I can't wait to get lost in the music and feel so sublime
I can't wait till this Friday since I'm going on a date
I can't wait till we're alone at night and...

TEACHER: okay Tony, thank you, I think we've heard enough for now

Clouds

Cumulus, cirrus and altostratus too

Clouds are the Creator's paintbrush

And the sky his illustrious canvas

The streaky cirrus up on high

The mountainous fluffy white cumulus hugging the Earth

And the dense cumulonimbus threatening to drench the ground

Clouds make the sky complete

Zeus the cloud gatherer looks on and smiles

As he paints ever-changing pictures throughout the day

Coalition

Not of their own volition
Would they have wanted to form a coalition

Now in need of erudition
So it doesn't turn into a battle of attrition

With the inevitable dissolution
And public statements of contrition

There has not been many a coalition government before
We all hope it will be stable and secure

Or the electorate will show them the door
And Labour will again return to the fore

Coffee machine machinations

I arrive at the coffee machine and wait in line for my double espresso. Lisa and Jill are in front of me chatting about a famous celebrity couple who have just separated because of the infidelity of the premier league footballer husband. I respond by stating how shocked I am at their split. Lisa replies by stating that the footballer is a typical man and that men will never change their cheating habits.

Lisa then reveals that she has been trying a new fad diet; she sweats buckets at the gym but all to no avail. I try to reassure her that she looks quite attractive and that she should give the diet a while to work. She does not seem convinced; she tells me instead that she wants to look like how she looked when she was twenty one and when lots of guys turned their heads when she walked along the street.

I tell her that she looks good for her age. Instead of consoling her my comment seemed to have made her agitated and annoyed. I try to change the subject but Lisa talks about cosmetic surgery and the various procedures she might like to undergo. I explain that we all will get grey hair and wrinkles some time and that it is natural. She disagrees and tells me about a Hollywood diva who has had undergone over twenty cosmetic procedures.

Claire arrives at the coffee machine and Lisa and Jill don't look pleased. Claire is a size eight, she can eat what she likes and she knows all the guys like her. I let all three of them chat while I read the text message I have just received on my mobile phone. I hear Claire saying that John had asked her out on a date. I gasp in disbelief because he is a partner at the law firm and I know this type of liaison is definitely not de rigueur. Claire looks at me and smiles smugly, Lisa and Jill look grim.

As Claire walks away with a new found spring in her step, Lisa and Jill look at her enviously and with a hint of disgust. I mention that Claire does get a lot of attention from men. I find myself at the receiving end of a tirade of abuse directed at size eight women, the media and shallow men who want eye candy.

I apologise for mankind's shallowness and make a swift exit claiming that I have a meeting in half and hour. I say my temporary farewell to the coffee machine, knowing that the caffeine craving will return later.

I sit at my desk and wonder what it would be like to be a coffee machine, privy to the multitude of stories, secrets and bits of juicy gossip that its users extirpate whilst they are on their coffee break.

Conscript

Conscript to the nation

Conscript to the company

Conscript to the body

Conscript to the mind

Conscript to conceived perceptions

Conscript to received suggestions

Conscript to quarks and m bosons

Conscript to societal memes

Conscript to familial relations

Conscript to political expediency

Conscript to the vagaries of bureaucracies

Conscripts to delays in public transport

Conscript to sunny climes

Conscript to winter blues

Conscript to past and the future

Conscript to the unknown.

Enlisting now.

Creative commons

Toddlers in the paddling pool kicking away with glee

Rabbits in the field burrowing and gnawing away enthusiastically

Raindrops on the greenhouse roof creating an ever-changing symphony

Foxes scampering over garden fences leaving their scents along the way

Red robins perching on branches and pausing to look around

Workmen humming tunes to themselves whilst listening to the radio

Pedestrians crossing the road and rushing here and there

Shoppers grinning with delight after buying an item they've always wanted

Couples locked in passionate embraces and staring meaningfully at each other

Lovers reunited after being separated by time, distance and work

Friends catching up and enjoying a well deserved night out

Stag, hen and birthday party revellers painting the town red, gold and green

Credit Crunchie

It's called a crunch but it hurts a bunch

When out to lunch or paying for fruit punch

It hits us all and makes us squeal

When we can't afford our very next meal

A recession busting cocktail is the medicine to calm

A tonic to raise supply and demand will work a charm

'The credit crunch' is such a gracious euphemism, so elegant and disarming

It justifies the excesses without causing alarm

Passed off as the inevitable result of counter-cyclical tendencies

So society should forgive and forget, and wait for the next boom like lackeys

When the next boom inevitably does appear

We'll all forget and irrational exuberance will reappear

And once again the curtain will eventually fall

The good times will stall; they'll be no prom ball

And next time around they'll be no-one to call, we'll all just fall

Like Humpty from off the wall, and end up getting mauled

By a financial tsunami of self-combustion

Resplendent economic waves of creative destruction

Not the dot com, tulip, or south sea mania

They'll invent another euphemism to take us all back into insania

Much better then to turn it into a boom and bust edible chocolate kite

It melts in the mouth and tastes a delight

It goes down well at all times of day

And whatever the cost, it's a price we'll all be willing to pay

Cycling

Far away on a mountain path, three cyclists made a tryst with fate

Fear not fair miss for there shall be no fee

Instead a passing breeze that carries a song for thee

The wind whispered the itinerary for the day

A short trip to Wimlands and St. Leonard's

Or a round-trip excursion to Shoreham by Sea

The sun danced and the wind moaned gently

And so we headed south

On the six-stage Downs Link way

At last lying down on Shoreham beach

Exhausted and dehydrated, but feeling like life's a beach

I close my eyes, the sun dances on my eyelids

A little while later I open my eyes

And I see white fluffy clouds smiling at me

They hold the key to the perfect Turner landscape

The wind is gentle

Too gentle to invigorate sweaty and tired cyclists

The sun is like an electric blanket covering me loosely

Why are such fine days so few and far between?

If only I can create a weather machine
Then I need to dream no more of glorious sunny days
For they will appear at my whimsical behest

I drift again into sweet reverie
Of cycle tracks
And country pub snacks

Of journeys through fields and meadows
Of farmers harvesting their crops
And sheep grazing and lazing

Of crossing train tracks and unmanned crossroads
Of the many roads without cycle tracks
Of the hole in my CamelBak

A strange tingly sensation emerges
Spreading from my feet to my head
I become quite light in the head

[Perhaps hypoglycaemia combined with minor amnesia]

I dream of being served Lucozade
By beautiful brunette and blonde ladies
While lying under palm trees relaxing in the shade

Too much cycling and too little food

Has left me dreaming

Of edible rose bushes

And marzipan streets

With chocolate street signs

And plastic water bottles made of candy

Of Evian water cascading down tree trunks

And hot roast potatoes on silver plates near river banks

And tulip shaped flutes filled with irresistible fruit punch

Daydreaming

Daydreaming of you

As I drift along the sea

The horizon melting like butter

The sun pulsing through the cerulean sky

The empyrean vault opens and overflows

Streams of synaesthesia hallucinating before they sublimate

A champagne toast is needed to celebrate the ubiquitous human allegory

Since halcyon days are back again

Dear Alice

Dear Alice
Living in your palace
Without any malice
Drinking from the silver chalice

When you look through the looking glass what do you see?
Do you see a thousand suns or an ocean colour scene?

So peaceful and at home in your glorious wonderland
Happily enjoying utopian adventures

So far from mendacity
Tis the place that leaves you with perspicuity

Can you take me to your secret hideaway?
The place you go to getaway

Dieting

All these new diets in glossy magazines claim that I will slim fast

I have tried some in the past

And most leave me feeling aghast

Nevertheless, I may give it a blast

And see how long I can last

But the diet that involves eating tapeworms does seems like a mighty task

Don't' get greedy

When your stocks have gone up

When you're three goals ahead

When you've gambled and won

When you are ahead in the race

When you're eight lives down and feel you have eight more left

When you're reaping the fruits of your hard work

When you're living life to the full

When everything is going your way

Don't get greedy.

Do you?

Do you have what it takes to please me?
Do you have what it takes to tease me?
Do you have what it takes to keep me?
Do you have what it takes to keep me happy?
Do you have what it takes to keep me fulfilled?
Do you have what it takes to keep me yours forever?

Do you think you know what it takes to please me?
Do you think you know what it takes to tease me?
Do you think you know what it takes to keep me?
Do you think you know what it takes to keep me happy?
Do you think you know what it takes to keep me fulfilled?
Do you think you know what it takes to keep me yours forever?

Dragon's Den

<u>INSTRUCTIONS:</u>

ENTER THE DEN WITH ALL YOUR INVENTIONS

NEGOTIATE A DEAL AND YOU ARE A WINNER

<u>WARNING:</u>

THE DRAGONS MAY BREATHE OUT TORRENTS OF FIRE SO
MAKE SURE YOU ARE MADE OF STEEL

Dream partner

A pop star, film star, sports star or the boy or girl next door

From puberty to the present moment there must have been a few

Most of the time it is someone you know but they're out of reach

Sometimes it's someone you've never met but would like to meet

Sometimes it's not your current partner but let's keep that fact hidden

If the universe delivers what you wish for then you'll end up with your dream partner

Drifting

My signs are critical
Just cut the cord and let me drift

It'll be swift
To the crypt

Follow me into the Sun
For one day Elysium awaits!

But not yet, rest easy Charon, exalted boatman of the Styx
For ye must wait while I elope once more!

White lights flash
My life swims past

Like a phoenix I arise
Cats envious of the many lives I possess

I see a red London bus I travelled to school on
I see the wild surf at Waikiki

Finally I see the gates and I smell the sweet lavender
For now Elysium calls me home.

Dual Identity

So you're Chinese and British, who exactly are you?

So you're Indian and British, who exactly are you?

So you're Greek and British, who exactly are you?

So you're Irish and British, who exactly are you?

So you're Jamaican and British, who exactly are you?

So who exactly are you? British and proud is what she said.

Education

A second	Is not enough to learn anything at all
A minute	Is enough for a cursory glance at a few pages of text
An hour	To understand the substratum of the entire tome
A day	To digest and mull over what I read today
A week	And now I'm ready to be examined on Voltaire
A year	To put into practice what I have learnt so far
A decade	And now I'm a graduate of the University of Life
A lifetime	Of success and failures, the learning never ceases…..

Emergency room

You're in the emergency room late at night, what a surreal place to be

Pumped full of morphine to ease the pain and infused with remicade constantly

You're being given i/v's in each arm, then ecg's and numerous other tests

Little do you realise the activity, flurry and mayhem that you've caused in this intensive care fest

You're told you're having a heart attack and that you may not make it through the night

Such a bizarre unexpected turn of events that leaves you full of fright

Suddenly, the mad scramble around you disappears and an eerie silence emerges

Because you're now floating high above your physical body, in the land of the unicorns and mythical flying horses

It's cold, it's hazy and there's a claustrophobic white light shining down and entombing you

There's a crystal clear river flowing underneath you and green pastures permeate your view

You're scared but you're calm, equanimous and lost in solemn contemplation

The grim reaper has come to visit, his metier since the first days of creation

Eminem

Oh yeah, ere we go y'all
Rabbit skip, Rabbit trip but Rabbit never quit

Got some herb, on the kerb, straight from the 'burb,
Hear the verb; glide that curve, n feel the swerve

Got my props, got my rocks and all the ice
Rhymes so sweet, rhymes divine, rhymes tastes like spice

Rhymes that echoes down the years
Tis is time that all the generations hear

Drop that prejudice, drop that fear cos I've got no time to care
Only time to dare so let the whole world hear

Simple, straight, ain't no time to front
Feel the rhyme n feel the beat enthralling you in your seat

Musical smorgasbord flow from the heart
Straight to the top of the Billboard chart

Drink it up, sip it up n gulp it down
Energise, realize n play it loud

Emotional IQ

Once we were savages
But now man dwells in the midst of the city
Living peacefully in the urban jungle
As his emotional circuitry develops civility

Yet every now and then
When enraged, threatened or provoked
A spark of rage and the battle cry of long ago is heard
And you again see glimpses of the savage

Endless Love

Whether near or far

Wherever you are

You will always be my shining twinkling star

Even though sometimes we may be apart

You are always in my heart

My one and only sweetheart

Every night I dream of us laughing, drinking Baileys and eating candy

On a beautiful white beach that's warm and sandy

Having lots of fun and being together completely free like a bird that flies like a grandee

I am always here for you in the good times and the bad, whether you are happy or sad

We will overcome all and forever be glad

I love you more with each moment that passes, with each breath I take, with each day that is had

My heart beats together forever with yours as one

Our souls unite and glow with peace, harmony and fun

Your love warming me like the rays of the morning sun

I've found in you my sweet love

An endless love

That shines so bright like the moon and stars in heaven above

Envoi

Prince! As the curtain falls on the theatre of life

May the voice of poets echo through the aisles and through the streets

May the Muse continue her fateful journey

And release her treasured bounty

Each poet now a star twinkling high up in the heavens

Orbiting in the ether

Dancing with angels

At one with the Logos, Ain Soph Aur and Brahman

Epiphany

Tracing the residue of a night between the sheets

I see our clothes crumpled on the floor

Each moment we shared you made me feel like I could walk on water

A love that rose like a volcano from the depths of the ocean

We inhabited an island paradise filled with laughter and love

Love can move mountains, conquer the unconquerable and make the impossible possible

Epitaph

1 TIMOTHY 6:12

Eudaimonia

Escaping Marxist self-alienation

And the confines of Plato's cave

I bask in the incandescent sunlight

Forgetting a world in a state of anomie

Sidestepping Kant's Rubik's cube

And Descartes' duality

I march onwards revelling in Hegel's spirit and Zarathustra's magic

Until I reach an euphoric state of eudaimonia

Eulogy

Whether it was or wasn't meant to be

C'est la vie

Event horizon

The next big task comes into view

And the clock ticks down to the event horizon

It is still far away but I'm psychologically prepared

The rays of the approaching Sun now blistering the skin

The day draws near and it is filled with excitement and dread

The only option is to break through the horizon and hit the
ground running

A temporary sense of relief as things turns out difficult but a
little easier than expected

Until the next big event horizon comes into view

Exam time

The joys of exams tickle me not

Like an unforgettable bundle of pleasure and pain

Try as I like I will forget them not

As the exam draws near the wheels of grey matter are dusted down again before reporting for action

Condensing and refining my notes like I'm adding finishing touches to a Picasso

Boiling it down to the essence and then boiling it down again some more

Never too sure if I've done enough exam prep

Cognisant of all avenues that may be pursued

Always thinking of a golden nugget that will raise my grade

It's a race to the windows aisle, so please do not contest

A window seat is my target and only tunnel vision will do

It is the oasis in the desert that promises to quench my thirst

A seat with a view is an exam's golden ticket

From there I can relax and enjoy my three hour vista

Sun, rain, clouds, birds, blimps, I've seen them all

Pilot, Stabilo and Uni-ball are the brushes

The essential tools of the exam trade

The answer booklet my unopened and untouched canvas

I look out of the window and let my mind wander away

A moment to reflect and think what to write

A moment to energise as I get back to work

The invigilator calls as the long hand of the clock strikes the hour

And exams papers are opened in eerie silence

I enter the zone and tunnel vision ensues once more

A cough here and a request to go to the loo there

Time to focus and have a quick look at the clock

Tick tock, an hour has already gone by

Now I wish time would pass so much slower

But no time to start wishing

I become an automaton again

A tough question confronts me sardonically

Like a stranger in a dark narrow alley

No where to turn and no where to hide

Aficionados of Schadenfreude smile but I face the question head on

Stuck in a hole where there is no possible escape

I scavenge for an answer, like a prospector for gold

The vultures swarm above me but I will not retreat

Never studied speleology but I will find a way out

No time to prevaricate, I exclaim Geronimo instead

I'm a master of disguises so I plan an audacious escape

My ability for savoir-faire means I salvage and extemporize

From the jaws of defeat I rise to my feet

Not a moment to waste, it's time to act with haste

Fasten the seatbelts and buckle down the hatches

Sweat rolls down my face as the last bolt is latched

At last it is over

And I breathe sighs of relief

Tis time to celebrate and rejoice

Facebook

Give me the face
And the book
Then give me loads of friends
That I don't even know

A new way to keep in touch
Or a new way to idle away time
The social networking phenomenon
Gripping the ipod generation

Archbishop Rowan Williams may not like things that are fleeting
Preferring real encounters to online ones
But I am sure he will accept your friend request
If you send him a personalised greeting

A new competition with my friends has emerged
We compete fiercely to be the one with the most friends
Since this supposedly dtermines who is the most popular
A verification of who is the most valued and most admired

My face can be read just like a book
Or have you just read my updated Facebook status message?
I'll have to ramp up my privacy
If I get too many hocus-pocus messages

I thank you all for those birthday wishes
But I must get on and wash those dishes
Oh! Too many invites to great events
But I must get on and wash those dishes

It's late on a weekday night
And I get a curious urge to log on
No new messages, wall posts or friend requests
But another half hour wasted fulfilling the Facebook urge

The star sign page says I am a starfish
Another that I look like Pogo
I'm superpoked here and I return a superpoke there
Eventually I graduate to a new superpoke level

In my Facebook world I rule supreme
The world is as I want
I control who sees what and who does what
I'm the master of my domain

It may only be my profile
A glimpse into my world
But being my friend is a privileged thing
Not to be taken lightly

If you write an offensive wall post
Or try to flirt lewdly with any of my friends

You've committed an offence for which there is only one sentence
You'll be defriended in an instant

In my hay days of popularity
I've messaged loads of people
Then the powers that be warn me I'm messaging too much
And they'll ban me from the site

Other times I've added lots of friends
And the powers that be get angry at me
Instructing me to slow down
Or they will ban me from the site

What if Facebook is in fact a government creation?
Used to delve into the lives of the global nation
You're never safe with surreptitious big brother
A law unto itself always tearing up the Charter

Synthetic friendships and long distance acquaintances
Status updates and photo tags
Mafia wars and vampire raids
The new addiction gripping the global nation

Fame

Isn't it a shame

How everyone today wants to be famous?

A few rise to the top and spend a few moments in the limelight

Most then slide down the slippery pole into the perpetual twilight

Many think it's worth the fight to be famous

To be forevermore a sought-after entity like Elvis

Selling their soul to the devil for a few nickels

Since they're so fickle

For a minute

They feel like the sky is the limit

Until they get hit with hypocrisy and negative publicity

The downside of being a celebrity

Fast food poetry

The world is moving faster

My poetry is getting even faster

The world is 24/7, razzmatazz, glitz and glamour

My poetry is perennial, without the trimmings or the
somnambulistic clamour

The world is yearning for everything ten minutes ago, without
all the queues but with all the trimmings and mouth watering
flavours

My poetry is unpredictable, unadulterated, unrestrained,
unpackaged and for all to savour

The world is making more demands on everyone's time so that it
seems that everyone is always running out of time

My poetry is timeless, an entrée, main course and dessert all in
one, to be ingested anytime

The world is craving for the ultimate, instant fix-it-all solution

My poetry is the stress-free, organic, alternative solution

Ferya

From a moment of distress there came a dazzling angel of light

Bringing good news and happy insight

Absence does make the heart grow fonder

Being apart only makes true love grow stronger

Intrepid biomedical scientist striving both day and night

Polymath skills that amaze like an eagle in flight

Warm, caring and pure in heart

Gracious, compassionate and very smart

Soulmates once found are bonded for life

Your heart and soul feel like they are flying high like a kite

Through the good and bad times and through any strife

Salih and Ferya forever happy, Forever together, forever reaching new heights

First love

You are like heaven
On a cold and barren Earth

You are like nirvana
That lifts me to the outer strata

You are the chand and sitare
A love so pure and sincere

Flash Trading

The computers stir into a mesmerising rhythm

Using an elongated complicated algorithm

That is way too complex for me to fathom

Making money in a flash

To build up a stash

Of lovely delectable cash

Specialised armies of adrenaline junkies looking to make big
money

Using high frequency trading, now so much more seductive than
a Playboy Bunny

Billions made and lost in a flash until the next big crash, fuelled
by the insatiable love of delicious money

Flowers

These flowers are sent with love

For a sunshine angel sent from heaven above

In the good times and the bad, in sickness and in health, whether you are happy or sad

I will stand by you always until I see you once again glad

Wherever you are, whether near or far

My heart is with you, my shining twinkling star

If you ever worry or get upset

Imagine us singing Mariah and Luther's duet

I see us sooo happy again whenever I dream

Laughing and drinking Baileys and eating ice cream

My love, I hope and pray you get well soon

And again enjoy the beauty of gazing at the twinkling stars and full moon

Food shopping

Another trip to the supermarket
Lost in queues
Buying more food than I expected to

I never go food shopping when hungry
Since my eyes grow bigger
And my stomach grows hungrier

I eventually end up shopping for food online
Being tempted by the special offers
And still buying more than I wanted to

For my dogs

Running through Sutton Common Park chasing other dogs
Out in all weathers: sun, rain and snow

Not listening when called but following their noses
Strutting their stuff and a variety of poses

Monty Lou, so wise and true
The golden Labrador, the soldier dog who fought the good fight

Cooper Mayo, so playful and so naughty
Sadly missed, never forgotten

Their sixth sense and intelligence always astounded
As did their keen sense of smell and their dogged
determinedness

Man's canine brothers, man's best of friends
What would man possibly do, without his four legged brethren?

A dog is for life, not just for Christmas
Dogs always give unconditional love in the good times and the
bad

For all dogs worldwide and those that have passed
A fellowship of goodwill, salute!

FOUR

Fortune favours fearless fusiliers

Over obsequious orators

Uttering useless

Rhetoric

Further

The further one goes from oneself

Into lands of make believe and surreal imagination

The more one suffers from alienation

And the dilution of one's mental faculties

The further into oneself one ventures

Into self knowledge and self mastery

The more one grows externally

Eventually reaching harmony with the inner self

Global Inception

It all started with a noble idea

That was put in the air
That then entered the stream
Then floated into the ether

And then into peoples hearts
And changed their minds
And society began to move

To a better tomorrow.

Goddess

The yin, the feminine
Laminate and mutable

A face that launched a thousand ships
And spawned the future kings

The fairer of the species
The goddess who can make man do extraordinary as well as
stupid things

As man yearns for feminine affection and fruits of the loom
Mesmirised by the face that launched a thousand ships and
spawned the future kings

The goddess gives man life
And makes life worth living

If only all men would treat all women
As the goddesses they rightly are

Hand of Fate

Oh Hand of fate, ye Janus faced Mandala
Bringer of fortune and of woe
Living life like Odysseus in Homer's Odyssey
So close to Ithaca but yet so far

Roll with the decisions and blows
Where it's going to take you, no one knows
Go with the flow
Fate, make it your mate

Harry Potter

Can't seem to shake the resemblance
To Hogwarts most valiant one

My glasses are too similar
If only I had his magical powers

Healthy body and healthy mind

Exercising in the aerobic zone trice a week
Makes me feel alive and at my peak

Mediation and yoga combine to liven the encephalon
I feel like King Arthur on the Fortunate Island of Avalon

Hearts at melting point

I'm in a different place, we're not compatible
We want different things, we're too different
We need to talk, we should take a break
This is not working out, there is something missing

Something deep inside dies every time love is forsaken
Some build up defences and others carry emotional scars
The flames of love simmer until once again they are rekindled
Love returns to full bloom and dispels all the gloom

Help Haiti

A concrete mausoleum, my throat so dry
Can't feel my legs, my eyes are sore
Not drunk or eaten in days, will I survive?
How long will it be before someone rescues me?

I've lost the concept of time down here
My mind drifts in and out of consciousness
Can't move at all, can't see at all
The silent darkness surrounds me like a velvet glove

Alone and still, the mind wanders again
My life flashes by, just pictures in the mind
Searing hot pain courses through my veins
My life force weakens with every hour that passes

If this is my last stand, then make it quick
Can't swallow anymore, my throat too parched
My eyes can't open, it takes too much energy
In my mind I sing songs to numb the pain and nothingness

Far away someone must hear my call
Closer to God now than ever before
If He is calling me home then I am now ready to return
Finally to be at peace and experience no more pain

Awoken forcefully, bright lights shine in my eyes

Foreign voices speaking, is this a dream or am I in heaven?

A sip of water, an intravenous feed and I slowly regain my bearings

I've been rescued at last, what a miracle this is

Hilltop Castle

In the distance the blissful snow capped peaks promise so much

A future of serene tranquillity and mountain fresh air

Yet each castle turret faces all four corners of the earth

Testament to the thunderous Napoleonic visions that once were writ large

A rusted well used sundial captures a time of yesteryear

When swords clashed with swords in high altitude fields of lavender

Conifer trees rise all around and mask the history

When fresh blood spilled on crispy brown leaves

The whistling of the trees dancing to the gentle icy wind signals peace has returned

Total silence at night only broken by a distant owl's random hoot

History repeats itself

If you want to know the future

Look to the past

And you will see the simple pattern

History repeats itself

America now, China tomorrow, who will be the next
superpower after that?

Britain, Rome, Persia, Alexander, Genghis

The rise and fall of nations and empires

History repeats itself

A new alliance, a brand new treaty, a new regional group and a
new trade

organisation

A modus vivendi, a non-proliferation pact and a non-aggression
treaty

The usual agreements, posturing and manoeuvring

History repeats itself

Why look to the future when you can look to the past

The Janus faced god of fortune will take no prisoner

What once was, shall be and then shall vanish forever

History repeats itself

Another day done, the sands of time shift a little in the hour
glass of history

The book of history again filling up, a rising star here and a fallen hero there

Nostradamus' postulations doth predict

History repeats itself

Hogmanay

A passionate embrace, body against body, mouth against mouth

The fireworks we created more spectacular than Edinburgh's festive display

You sliding between my thoughts, drops of sweat trickling down your cheeks

Away from the festive cheer outside, our simple cheer as you caressed my face

Day dreams of you writhing and slithering between the satin sheets

Endless desire to feel the heat of your body close to mine

Holiday bounce

Relaxing carefree in a glorious tropical haven

A holiday can be the closest thing to heaven

Coming back to Heathrow after an amazing holiday

The high spirits and the sun tan reignites the holiday buzz and thoughts of fun and frolics

Forget the pep talk or the latest supermarket pick-me-up

Head to the sun or snow, fly short or long haul, just make sure when you go you live it up

The halcyon days are back again, a lifetime of uplifting memories and sweet foreign melodies

The holiday bounce leaves me swinging like the sixties

Holistic Philosophy

A philosophy must include a philosophy of life, work, parenting, civic responsibility, nature and the cosmos. They are all separate parts of an integrated whole.

Reading philosophy is not enough, only through application, through praxis, can one become. Philosophy can provide the signposts, each individual must then discover for themselves their own path, their own truth.

Sometimes it is only in moments of great despair or suffering when one understands their true essence. Other times it is in moments of great joy, achievement or exhilaration when one becomes whole again. There cannot be one standard formula. Philosophy is only the foundation; the house must then be built brick by brick by each individual.

Everyone is the master of their own destiny. Most individuals do not know what their final house will look like, their dreams are only the blueprint. Then as their house takes shape and the years roll by, the individual has another revelation: their house will never be finished. Life's journey never ceases and learning never stops. At this point many start to live in the moment rather than in the past or in the future.

Sometimes one's house is shaken to the core; sometimes it is raised to the ground. In these times of perceived misfortune one understands that life is never certain, it is always changing. One sees the fragility of life and the futility of clinging to order and certainty. In this moment of chaos each individual finds that there is indeed something that is permanent, that something is love. As they swim in the ocean of love, all suffering, fear and worry melts away.

As each individual then realises that the sands of time will one day wash away the house they have built, they then learn that they are more than the sum of their current lived existence. They are part of the universal whole, timeless and infinite.

Hollie

Life stands still when you walk past
The heart beats ever so fast

The die is cast
Can't we stop this moment and make it last?

Overflowing with beauty, joy and radiance that no one can
constrain
A princess spreading rays of sun through the falling rain

A gift from god to behold
A story yet to unfold

My wish still remains untold
To come in from out of the cold

It is my heart that feels so true
But when will I feel less blue

You make me smile
And raise my temperate a few notches up the dial

A ray of light
That shines so bright

Your hypnotic smile and friendly glance was all it took to leave me entranced

And now I'm forever enchanted by your seductive trance

Hollywood Dream Team

Hit the deck
develop those pecs
time to check
flip flopping
hip hopping
quick talking just ain't good enough

Silver screen dream
time to generate income streams
let the gold, silver and diamonds sparkle

Dazzling through the crystal meth haze
step out of the daze
and you'll find a way out of life's maze

You wanna get paid and laid
be in the limelight and not in the shade
never to fade like the Florida everglades

Nobody got it made
it's about hard work, luck and always being staid
so get out of your domestic cage
and hit the international stage

You may think you're the real deal

but this ain't no fairy tale, this is for real

It's all up to you

so what you gonna do?

Hollywood is where your heart is

Hollywood is what you dream of

There's gonna be a tussle

when you bust your Los Angeles hustle

with the hope of making Hollywood bustle

Hong Kong

The sweet smell of jasmine invigorating Victoria Peak and the spectacular views

The carbon emissions of the city and the hustle and bustle of people and traffic

The fresh produce of the market, such seafood delights

The salty fog drifting across Victoria Harbour amidst the luxurious yachts

The luminescence of the neon lights making the night seem as bright as day

Timeless and memorable, a visit to Hong Kong in the spring

Icarus

Flying too close to the sun is in my nature

Re-rooting the source to get out of danger is now part of the
mixture

Resurrection, insurrection and not enough contemplation

Too close for comfort, too close to call, yet another conflagration

Nerves of steel always get tested to the limits

In the end returning to nature and the sanctuary of the sonnets

Rising in the east to the sound of Long Tall Sally

Setting in the west sipping Bacardi on the beach whilst enjoying
a dally

Living in the age of machines, echoes of infallibility reverberate

As mankind fights pitch battles with nature

In the twenty second century, Icarus, now a man-made jet

Will fly daily to the space station housed in Earth's outer orbit

Ice age

Will the gulf winds switch and leave Western Europe in a new
ice age?

Catastrophic conditions befalling millions and millions
Blizzards every day and freezing nights
We all will be prisoners in the Arctic's frozen cage

Riot and wrath will ensue in the internecine fight for survival
Malthus may be proved right
As Schumpeter's waves of creative destruction flummox us all

If only?

How did I know we'd be friends from the start

Closer than siblings we will never be apart

Coffee breaks and laughs to keep the LPC from making us cower in the dark

Our conversations will always be more inspiring than a work of art

Escaping from the confines of the Little Titchfield Street ramparts

Until we find a place in the sun that brings joy to the heart

Imagine a world where...

We'd love each other irrespective of differences in age, cast, creed, race, disability, sexual orientation and religion

There will be enough food, clean water, shelter and jobs so everyone could live peacefully, blissfully and in harmony

There would be no pain, suffering, disease and hunger

There would be renewable energy supplies that didn't blight the

landscape and didn't destroy the rainforest

Animals and all living creatures would be treated with the dignity and respect they deserve

And the world will be for one and all to share, without division, barriers, and exclusions

Inner citadel

Life is short
So live it sweet
And spread the love

Make virtue your bastion
Hope your bulwark
And faith your fortress

In remembrance

Remembering all of a life once lived

In hope and in the foothills of the seven storey mountain

Hark! Mount Olympus is beckoning

Gregorian chanting in the garden of Gethsemane

Remembering darkness turned to light

Remembering the good times

As I turn my tears into smiles

Rejoicing for each happy moment we shared

A fortiori! Continuing onwards on life's precious journey

And along each mile I'm still carrying a smile

Insania

Sententious hypocrites still possess the narcissist trait
Constant conflagration burns daily within them

Each moment of madness tests the sanity of their vanity
Each pinch and burn reminding them they are still mortal

Inside the ring

The c h a l l e n g e

The f o c u s

The a d r e n a l i n e r u s h

The s h o u t s o f t h e c r o w d

The s w e a t

The b l o o d

The p a i n

Insomniac

Lying awake in the night when I'm too tired to fall asleep

Counting sheep eventually becomes a pointless and irritating feat

Dozing uncomfortably as the clock ticks slowly but incessantly on

Shapeless forms appear as I drift along, gripped by a freezing mist and without the energy to awake because my body feels like it weighs a ton

Too much caffeine has left me restless

Studying hagiography and Leo Tolstoy's tomes cannot placate the listlessness

My stomach growls as the hunger pangs grow implacably stronger

The more I beseech sleep the further it retreats into crevices unimaginably small, hidden in locked chambers far yonder

Feeling like a somnambulist drunk with drowsy mirages of slumber

Thwarted by the encephalon's opprobrium at forced slumber

Entreating the mind to holiday on the shores of the placid serene lake of deep sleep

Itinerant and skittish it superciliously elopes far from the ethereal goal of sleep

Internet Dating

An advert

Lawyer looking for love, I wont judge you but missing out on me will be criminal.

I want to be successful in my career but I also want to lead a balanced life; to spend time with loved ones and to experience the beauty that life has to offer. I am looking for a soulmate, someone I can connect with, have chemistry, share the good/bad times and be my best friend. Like yin/yang energy, where that special bond grows stronger each day.

I know we sometimes go through life at 100 miles an hour and we sometimes think we know what we want rather than what will truly fulfill us and make us truly happy. Any relationship takes time and commitment; and of course love, that special bond between two people that can make you feel a warm glow inside on the coldest and rainiest of days and where just the thought of that special person is enough to make you smile.

If you would like to learn more about me, drop me a message with contact info....

Ireland calling

The emerald isle bugle sounds in my ears
It is time to return to the land of dreams and merriment

The streets of Dublin are calling
The oyster festival at Clarinbridge is calling
The opera festival at Wexford is calling
A lunchtime stroll around Eyre Square is calling

A sail along the River Shannon is calling
St. Finbarre's cathedral in Cork is calling
King John's castle in Limerick is calling
A trip to the hurling final at Croke Park is calling

Discover Ireland, discover yourself

It is what it is

Everything is what it is
Life is a fluctuating cycle
Each moment only transitory
Each life an accumulation of moments

Step back from the torpor
And the constant accumulation game
Because in the end we're all the same
A pile of dust and bones

Ivory tower

Retreat to the ivory tower

The home of savants

And intrepid loquacious scholars

The place of ideas

Knowledge

And contemplation

The place of solace and perspicuity

I am a spermicid

I wallow away waiting for the time

That precious moment when I will be released in a river of steam

At last the eruption occurs and I travel along

Trying to outdo my competing brethren

The egg is the target

The bull's eye that I must impregnate

Big Phil had a go but the doorman said no

So he sulked and retreated keeping his head held low

Crazy Neil took a chance, full steam ahead with his lance

Hoping his shimmy shenanigans would fit the bill

Unfortunately for him he failed to impress

So he retreated in defeat, his tail between his legs

And now I get my turn so I coif my hair and straighten my clothes

I pass the first hurdle, the overweight bouncers

Now to fertilise the egg, it should be cinch

I let my load go and then roll over and fall fast asleep

I Believe

When I am weak, He is strong

I know not my destination, but I know He will guide me

When all is lost and in ruin, I Believe

When all hope is gone, I Believe

After all the wars, natural disasters, famines and plagues, I Believe

In the final hour, I Believe

I Spy

I spy with my little eye

You spy with your little eye

The dog spies with its little eye

The cat spies with its little eye

The bird spies with its little eye

The world spies with its little eye

Everyone spies with their little eyes.

Jack

Jack, Jack! the joker in the pack

Never left out on the rack

He's always in the shack

Full of beans and at a Heineken six pack

Jersey Sojourn

St. Helier sojourn awaits
Flapjacks, cookies and crumble on offer to entice

Rum, Kalua and Jaegermeister can't stifle the appetising trifle
Of the new perspective intravenously sprouting within you

Soufflé and hot chocolate deluxe
Will send your intestines into a mesmerising flux

Java City can offer a temporary re:treat
Far off from the pick-me-up, salty snack and ready packed
beaten track

Bristol Maid and her ubiquitous cloned sisters on hand to help
Generic accoutrements lining the floors and ceilings as far as the
eye can see

It don't feel like gravy and I wonder if it ever should have
More like a stint of porridge, your body locked down by the
hand of providence

Just one night

There is a buzz in the air tonight
Sparks fly in the glorious moonlight

I walk like royalty with my ice glittering bright
On top of the world, I glow in the twilight

The evening awaits like an open book
It'll be fun, resplendent and off the hook

KATZ

Twinkle, twinkle through the night

Agents that will leave you glowing with delight

Like enchanting birds in flight

Dazzling agents sparkling with diamonds and gold

Enamouring London in the hot sun and blistering cold

A dream to behold for the few who get to hold

Swiping a C6012X cipher to enter Room 4.12, the headquarters of
the troupe

Halcyon days of frolics and resplendent moments for all the
group

Crepuscular adventures forever crystallised in the cerebral soup

Keep things simple

The list of things we must achieve
By the time we're 30, 40, or 60
Becomes more and more every year that passes

If you haven't achieved any you're some kind of failure
Any even if you have that is never enough
For there is always someone who has achieved more

So keep things simple and forget all the hype
You are a survivor on Earth
You're already a winner

Knowing

To know God, one must know thyself
Through knowing God, one will know thyself

To become infinite, one must transcend the finite
To become a rishi, one must already know

Krishnamurti

Look not to the past
Look not to the future

An encounter with aloneness
Can elevate the mind to new terrains

In a state of constant awareness
There will be freedom from fear

Be an observer and w-i-t-n-e-s-s the reality
There is no journey, only the here and now

The observer is the observed
Go beyond fear to be free

Between space and silence, an inner richness
That invites new experiences and ways of living

Laissez-faire

Hidden from view, the invisible hand of the market wields its magic

The tide washes the deepest footprints of tradition away

Free will of the free market excites the buffalo herds

They roam and stampede through the bullring of the bourse

Hayek sails his kayak through the Keynesian everglades

The tall reeds reminding sailors of their lack of autarky

The evanescence of the laissez-faire spectre is swifter than a fleeing thief in the night

Until another spectre emerges and evolves, like a hybrid Caligula

Leela

Listening to the rhymes of Kabir, Rumi and Sanai
I drift back and remember sweet childhood memories
And the tender songs of innocence

Bedtime lullabies and fairy tales
That left me enchanted and left me feeling like I was a luminary

When each day I visited a new town
The world my playground

One day I was the sorcerer's apprentice
The next a soothsayer
And another day I was Charlemagne

Life in the womb

Sleeping for hours on end, life sustaining nutrients coming through my umbilical cord

So helpless, yet so free, so totally connected to my lifesource, my mother

I can feel each step she takes, I can sense when she is happy or sad

So little and yet so precious, I am a miracle of creation and a little bundle of joy for my parents

As I slowly grow inside her womb, feeding off all the nutrients and slowly wriggling about

I begin to feel more sensations, some exhilarating, some exciting and everything so very profound

I hear things but they all seem so strange, so new and so confusing

As my heart beats louder and louder, and as I grow more and more, I become closer and closer to my mother

The time approaches for me to leave my abode of nine months

I am really going to miss this warm, secure and safe environment

What waits for me outside I do not know, I feel fear and I am apprehensive as I find myself being pushed out

So here I go, at last I see the light, can hear noises and a lot of commotion, life in the womb was a very special time

Life on Deimos

Circling the red planet as the inanimate subordinate

The little brother of neighbouring Phobos

Captured by the colossus and its gravitational magnet

The unsymmetrical asteroid that once was thought of as dross

A life on Deimos beckons for intrepid space adventurers

Who aren't scared of surfing the perihelion or riding the Kuiper belt

They'll be the vanguard of Deimos' human colonisers

A brave new world built on craters and on Swift and Voltaire welt

Living on the crest of a wave

Living on the crest of a wave is the only way to live, says he

Show me how! Said she
Follow your heart and live without fear like me! Says he

How is that possible? Says she
Simple, be the best surfer you can be and ride the biggest wave like I do, says he

Can it be so simple? Says she
Life is complicated enough, so get back to basics and keep things simple, just go and enjoy the surf, says he

What if you crash? Says she
Life is an adventure, get your surf board out and surf; never worry! Says he

Which wave shall I choose? Says she
Life is like one big wave, before you know it it has gone so find the biggest wave and ride on its crest, say he

London Town rumours

People say this and people say that

About good ole' London town

That it's now too diverse or got even worse

Because of bankers and overpriced housing

But whatever they say

Tis the place I was born

Tis the place I do live

I will always love beautiful London town

They say it's too crowded

Too many cars on the roads

That it's not like it used to be

Maybe that is true and it can leave me feeling a little blue

When I'm stuck in a mile long traffic jam

But tis still is my city

So I battle on thru

I will always love beautiful London town

Looking at the stars

Some look to the church tower
Some look to the Eiffel tower
Others look to the stars

Some aim for the ceiling
Some aim for the sky
Others aim for the stars

Some are happy with the mundane
Some are happy with the extraordinary
Others are happy with the stellar

Some sit watching sit-coms on television
Some sit watching movies in the cinema
Others sit watching the stars

Some reach for the mountaintops
Some reach for the clouds
Others reach for the stars

Looking back

What would it be like if it was 2310 and I was reading this?

Would 2010 be considered a good year?

Will mobile phones and televisions be outdated?

And will virtual reality now be too real for some?

Will history look kindly on what we've done?

And did all of us living in 2010 do enough to ensure a better tomorrow for

others?

Looking forward

What will life be like
In the next millennium?

Will people live on Mars
And will the Earth still be inhabited by humans?

Will robots do all the work
And will humans live for hundreds of years?

Will cloning become the norm
And war a relic of the past?

Will famine and poverty be eradicated
And people fly around on pods?

Or will the Earth's population exceed twenty billion
And internecine struggle become de rigueur?

A post apocalyptic world
Where humans follow a path to self combustion

I wonder what new inventions will be thought of
And what new ways of living will emerge

What new modes of travel will develop

And whether love will still be the ultimate human emotion

I hope it will be a better world
And the Earths amazing eco system will still be intact

Where renewable green energy sources are used
And diseases are easily treated

But whatever will be, will be.

Los Angeles

Born in the city of angels
The east side rising

Waiter in the day
Actor in my dreams

Lying on Long Beach
And rollerblading along Venice beach

I'm Angelinos in spirit
Singing plaudits by the River of Babylon

Lost

Lost in the middle of St. Leonard's Forest

With only stinging nettles and brambles for company

Until out pops a rabbit that promptly scampers away

And a red squirrel retreats along the path it has come

Thirty three degrees and the afternoon heat burns my skin

Eventually I find a place of shade and relax in a starfish position

The sweet smell of jasmine and the gentle breeze embellish my tired loins

The thick layer of grass under my body, a delectable velvet mattress

Pondering what it will be like to spend a night in the forest

Water from the nearby stream whenever I am thirsty and a few berries for my dinner

Longing for the freshly made sumptuous sandwiches from the Black Horse Inn

Now even a mini snack from the supermarket seems like a luxury

My water bottle now empty

The parched earth providing no solace to the unprepared

As the sun slowly dips towards the horizon

I realise it will be pitch black soon so I gather my strength and continue

At last! I find my bearings as I come to a clearing
Parkminister in the distance and Whytings farm to the rear
West Sussex bridleways again got me in a pickle
My sense of direction temporarily proving much too fickle

Love constrained

Love constrained by custom

Love constrained by tradition

Love constrained by mores

Love constrained by social conditioning

Love constrained by religion

Love constrained by fear

Love constrained by jealously

Love constrained by selfishness

Love constrained by emotional baggage

Love constrained is never love unrestrained.

Love in the wilderness

I caught your glance
It became a spark
That lit a fire
And filled me with desire

We travelled the world
Across mountains and lakes
Watching the whole world unfurl
Still missing our African escapes

The early morning sun on the plains of the Serengeti
The warm gentle midday rain falling on our naked skin
The electric noise of the wildebeest as they head north on annual migration
The silhouettes of stately giraffes against the setting sun

I can see the universe
And our unborn children in your eyes
I can feel your love inside me
As I'm melted by your touch in the midst of the wilderness

Love of W.A.R.

Atomic warfare, chemical warfare, guerrilla warfare

Trench warfare, psychological warfare, technological warfare

Why can't humans just get along?

From long ago to eons ahead, man will fight with man no doubt

Victory can never be sweet; pain and death happens on both sides

Why can't humans just get along?

From the sands of the desert to the white snowy mountaintops

War sees no limit or boundary

Why can't humans just get along?

Innocent civilians, collateral damage

A means to an end, tactics, strategies and ambushes

Why can't humans just get along?

A new breed of warrior, a new kind of enemy

Technological savvy, non-nation state and always thinking one step ahead

Why can't humans just get along?

Looking at the Earth from the heavens above

The universe sees the constant unending conflagration of the nations

Why can't humans just get along?

Love's equinox

You are like a bluebird in the spring singing on the bodhi-tree

You are like a skylark in the summer dancing on the olive tree

You are like a red robin in the autumn chirping on the willow tree

You are like an Arctic tern in the winter perching on the chestnut tree

Low battery

When you least want it, when you least expect it

When you forget to charge it, when you're too busy to notice it

When you're away on holiday, when you've forgotten your charger

When you've played too many games, when you've browsed the net too much

When you're multitasking with multiple apps, when you're photographing all

the sights

When you've talked too much and not noticed that time has flown by

When you've texted too much and think one more text won't drain the battery

LPC

My mind wanders away from the speech on civil procedure

Distracted by the incessant strumming

Of the air conditioner in the lecture hall

The regulations and practice directions set my mind alight

Before the case law makes my insides rumble

Hunger pangs set in as I dream of irresistible slices of chocolate cake dripping with hot chocolate ganache

The workload hits me like an avalanche

A tsunami of case studies, accounts, precedents and mandatory rules

I sit back and relax on the La-Z-Boy recliner as the scented candle burns brightly at both ends

A unique experience testing the grey cells and the patience

Of even the hardened veteran of exams and coursework

A bitter sweet pill gladly swallowed to secure that elusive place on the roll

Lucozade

Thirst quencher
Giving succour to the three hundred pound bencher

Heading for a cramp
Until Lucozade revamps

Tired and sweating after forty minutes of spinning
Water just won't suffice, my taste buds revolting en masse

Only Lucozade entices
Super unleaded fuel for the muscles

Luminescence

In the flames of passion
Our souls collide and unite

Tonight shall be ours forever
As our bodies merge into rhythm

Beyond pleasure
Beyond nature's simple impulse

Ecstatic moans combine with cupid's harp concerto
Our bodies gliding together on the king size mattress

Our bodies alight
Our bodies luminescent

Lunch at the City of Westminster

"C'mon Jerry, let's go for lunch, it's half one and I'm famished" I say.

"To the cafeteria?" he asked, "no" I harked, "to the restaurant in Victoria Street."

So off we go, Jerry still trying to figure out the crossword at the back of his newspaper.

We meet O'Neill in the lift, "how you all doing?" he asks.

"We're good, just going for lunch" I say, Jerry looks up from his newspaper and smiles.

"Ok I'll come along, just give me a sec, I need to grab my coat."

Standing waiting at reception, my stomach starts groaning.

Along comes O'Neill, with Brian, Kerensa and Mark tagging along.

Off to the restaurant we go, we wait in line for a while until we're seated and chatting away.

"Did you see the match?" O'Neill asks me, "yeah of course I did, Chelsea did well with ten men. But what of United, they lost by a whisker and Liverpool have fallen into fifth spot?" We debate the latest developments in the Premier League.

The food finally arrives, fish and chips with peas and tomatoes, all steaming hot and looking a treat. We all tuck in ravenously.

"Brain is off on holiday to Thailand again," said O'Neill as he raises his glass of coke.

"Cool" I respond and I let Brian explain his love and fascination with the region "it's really swell, you'll love it there. Vietnam, Thailand, Cambodia and Laos are fantastic."

"He should be in sales, he's sold me already" I say to O'Neill.

Kerensa talks about growing up in New Zealand and Mark talks about life in Australia.

While sipping my tea I glance at my watch "it's time to head back to work guys" I say.

Jerry's crossword is almost done.

We trot back along the side street and have a look at the food shops and boutiques en route.

How time does fly when you are eating lunch, being merry and having fun at the City of Westminster.

Mandiba

A distant dream held long ago
Not for the faint of heart

You began the Long Walk decades ago
And still you walk today

A journey that at one time seemed so long
A journey that made you strong

The nation rejoices its very own
Your name will linger on

For what you've done to build anew
The nation rejoices in song

Man of the cloth

Just an ordinary man before
Now called to God by divine inspiration

A test of faith and inner being
A personal conversation with god

The beginning of a new spiritual union.

Mars

Welcome to Mars

A land where all your dreams can be fulfilled, but mostly they are not

Where 1 per cent of the population owns ninety-five percent of the wealth

Where the profit motive trumps the morality, fairness and compassion motive

Where greed is good and avarice is your best bedfellow

Where money is the only god, to be worshipped and coveted

Where wars can be profitable and life always has a price tag

Where everything has a price but never a value

Where you have to be in it to win it by any means necessary

Welcome to Mars.

Max

Live life to the max
Not Pepsi Max but Clifford, Max

Let him wield his magic wand
And a new life may have dawned

Lights, camera, action!
Pump up the volume, there's no option

Time to live life in the fast lane, high octane
Time to pop open the champagne

Maya

Life is a constant state of maya

Detach from your manacles

And merge into the river of consciousness

Accept change as inevitable, whether it is good or bad

Then you can live life to the fullest

Without fear or worry

Mean streets

The menacing look of high rise tower blocks
The harsh reality of the homeless lying rough
The needles and condoms littering the dark alleyway
The path with graffiti and broken street lighting

The constant smell of rot and decay
The boarded up shops and high unemployment
The grimace of those who live with no hope
The pain of those living hand to mouth

The mean streets is not someone else's problem
The mean streets won't simple vanish and disappear
The mean streets and its causes must be faced and rectified
The mean streets need not be mean at all

Migraine

Lightening strikes but I am still feeling fine

Then the rain pelts down and I feel the pain

The thunder claps loudly and my head aches

The earth shudders underneath and all forms of light now pierce
my skin

I lie down to rest and long for the storm to cease

But it is growing in intensity and about to reach its climax

So I reach for the paracetamol and codeine

And an hour later the storm passes my burrow

Mind of the ninja

The mind of the ninja is an extraordinary sight

Machinations, formulas and strategies that tempt and delight

A virtual computer that's programmed to fight

A Ninja will fight with all its might

You may resist or surrender but you will never see another daylight

Mittal

It ain't brittle, it's made of Mittal
Tough as steel and full of beans
Stainless and painless, the silver stuff brightens
It glimmers and glistens, it's not simply Mittalic

A cognate magnate, a cast iron guarantee
From Noah's Ark to Arcelor, a stellar parlour
When I was little I used to play with skittles
Now I enjoy the creative productions of Mittal

Mnemosyne

Dali's Persistence of Memory invites

Delving into memories clear and bright

What is life but a memory?

That lingers somewhere in the night

Of all those moments of joy exalt

More glimpses in the rear view mirror

Each fleeting joy or trouble passed

Accumulates as a remnant in the cerebral vault

Modern grammer

Modern grammer can b wot ever u want it to be

It can be liberating to not give a monkey's

Cos modern grammer ain't wot it used to be

It now can b wot ever u want it to be, init

Moonlight benediction

Yes Lord
Just you and me

In the cold of the night
Guided by the dim moonlight

I fall to my knees and call out your name
In my times of distress I feel you touch my heart

In my times of despair
My prayers I know you hear

Still my heart sometimes grows weak
I wonder if you will forsake me

Please forgive my transgressions
And my occasional vacillating heart

My spirit remains resolute
I know you will guide me through

Morden Park

Relax far away from the nearby suburban frenzy

A sanctuary overlooked by the commuting mêlée who pass it daily

Have a picnic, play golf and cricket, swim or marvel at the magnificent London skyline

Or have a workout at the Green Legacy Outdoor Gym and refine your waistline

The unknown 'Central Park' of South West London

Off the tourist trail and still an unspoilt Garden of Eden

Morley's Fried Chicken

Give it a go and you'll be pleasantly surprised
After a long night out partying Morley's is advised
A chicken burger and fries for one pound ninety nine
It tastes delicious and soaks up all the moonshine

Fly their wings with some barbecue sauce and French fries
A good deal to be had so long as you don't count the calories
Play the outdated slot machine if you need a break
Or look around and see the flurry of people passing through
from daybreak

Mount Snowdon

When I was little I went to climb Mount Snowdon (the tallest mountain in England), I was with my parents and sister. We got there early and the Sun was slowly rising, we took a rack and pillion railway up the mountain to the summit station.

The rack and pillion railway was amazing, the train chugs along slowly, puffing out smoke and the views on either side of the carriage are spectacular. Luckily it was a clear day, so we were able to see quite far and we were able to see the top of the mountain ahead. Sometimes the track passes along the edge of the cliff and beyond was a really steep precipice, so we held our breath and hoped the train was robust and there were no earth tremors.

From the summit station, we had to walk the rest of the way by foot, mostly the path is made up of slabs of concrete but as we climbed higher, the path shifted to gravel and then to snow and ice. The cloud cover began to hug us all around like a giant white duvet and the temperature dropped as the air thinned out.

On the way down, after stopping for a ready prepared sandwich and cottage cheese luncheon, the Sun started its descent and the golden rays spread across the horizon, the sky a myriad of red and orange. It was only when the Sun finally set that I realized why I wore so many woolies.

Mouse

I eat like a mouse, but I ain't no slouch

I gets da cheese, it's such a breeze

Yeah I love sleaze, so keep tabs on ya girl

Or I'll take her from ya

Too much rivalry, not enough cavalry

You can't handle another crusade

Lyrical finesse, that ya can't contest

Da superlative, south London spectacular

Streetwise vernacular, always avoiding the south circular

Driving, igniting, give me some nitro

It's now or never, cos forever is only a daydream

And I only live life in the fast lane, cos dats da only thing
keeping me sane

I ain't no Gnostic, intrepidly supersonic, always send ya cosmic

Double jeopardy, I gots da remedy

Ain't jumping on the next bandwagon; or the next tower of
babel, so keep ya

fable

I keeps it stable, fully able, always travel lite, no preconception
or conception

Ain't gonna judge ya, just gonna crush ya, lyrically

Fuelled by Jesus, from the cradle to the grave, in stereo

I got a royal flush, empyreal trophy, and I'm just a mouse

Murphy's Law

The verdict is in, you've been sentenced again

It's twenty five to life, with no chance of parole

An accidental fall and the mirror topples and shatters, it looks
like a porcelain animal that you have just slain

Seven years of bad luck or that's what you've been told

You step up to the plate preparing yourself for the next pitch

You've been dealt another screwball, it now looks like you've
been screwed again

No time to moan or feel down in the dumps, or you may end up
lying face down in the ditch

So get on with it and don't look back since you are your ship's
helmsman

Put your pedal to the metal, cast misgivings aside

Sail forth and forthwith, let the trade winds blow through your
sails

Keep focused, keep calm, keep swimming against the tide

Your limits are self-imposed and your reality based on
perception, not Murphy's hackneyed tales

A man's character is determined by how resilient his spirit is and
his willingness to thrive with endless drive

Don't pull any punches or live life by halves for only the brave will thrive

My England

Oh land of my birth
Land of endless beauty

I yearn for thee when I'm far away
And embrace thee with glee when I return home

Far and wide our influence has spread
To go where others have feared to tread

A certain benevolent character and a certain pride
That maketh this the greatest land

Yes I take thee beloved England
To love and die for

In sickness and in health
Till death do I depart

Forever be great and glory undimmed
Above all, this land, My England

My laptop

[23:00:16] Chandler: psychic laptop?

[23:00:30] Aphrodite says: no fast track one

[23:00:49] Chandler says: really fast track?

[23:01:00] Chandler says: where is track going?

[23:01:03] Aphrodite says: urs is really oldddddddddddddddiesssssss

[23:01:13] Chandler says: mine is powerful

[23:01:23] Chandler says: can transform into a human

[23:01:39] Chandler says: then can fly like a bird

[23:01:57] Chandler says: into the deep blue sky

[23:02:16] Aphrodite says: show me when it flies

[23:03:09] Chandler says: it flies so high and if you hold onto my laptop you will begin to feel like you can fly too

[23:03:46] Aphrodite says: ok let me see then

[23:04:16] Chandler says: ok, just sit back and relax, close your eyes and imagine....

[23:04:32] Chandler says: flying...

[23:04:51] Chandler says: in the sky...

[23:05:19] Chandler says: with the sun shining so bright and making you so warm

[23:06:00] Chandler says: the rays of sun penetrating you so deeply and powerfully as you fly so high

[23:06:43] Chandler says: the higher you fly the stronger the rays become

[23:07:41] Chandler says: penetrating each and every part of you

[23:08:20] Chandler says: until you feel so complete and fulfilled by the energy and are fascinated by the beauty

[23:09:07] Chandler says: so captivated by the colours and mesmerized by the views from being so high

[23:09:44] Chandler says: the air so pure and it tastes so fresh

[23:10:19] Chandler says: that you want to stay there forever...

[23:10:36] Chandler says: and ever...

My life as an ant

Running along doing my task for today
A stoic worker ant with a brimful of pheromones
Following my other brothers as I go on my way
Happy, merrily I sing and stridulate as I walk
Little do humans know what we ants do say
Most just crush us with the soles of their feet

Myself and the vespoidia are essential to the Earths biosystem
Messing with me and animalia will result in serious damage
I will spray you and bite you if you come near my ant colony
I will defend the queen with my life and summon the army ants
Millions of army ants will then swarm and attach you en masse
Fire ants and bulldogs ants will sting and destroy you

I don't like humanoids because they crush us ants, use pesticide
and destroy my habitat
I don't like anteaters because they try to eat me but I've always
evaded them
I don't like spiders; I'm a member of the arachnophobia club
I don't like caterpillars that try to trap me and eat ant larvae
I don't like ant birds, since they are predatory and mess with my
eusociality
I don't like brown bears, they are just big beasts who specialise
in klepto parasitic behaviour

My life as a bee

I'm a buzzing honeybee travelling all over the county

I've been to many places and I've pollinated many plants

A vibrant female worker bee ensuring the smooth functioning of the colony

Making the queen bee happy and keeping control of the drones

I forage around and ensure the safety of the colony

My sting is always primed with venom that is ready to unleash in kamikaze fashion

I hate being called a bee and much prefer to be called a bird

I hate apiculture and hide from the beekeeper in order to remain wild and free

I hate domesticated bees and always avoid being trapped in innovative artificial hives

I hate insecticides, pesticides and fertilizers

I hate climate change and colony collapse disorder

I hate the predatory giant hornets and I will swarm, sting and cook them in a heat-ball

My life as a flee

Shaken awake by the stirring of the mattress
My beauty sleep stolen by some hefty humanoid
I want revenge so I jump and cling to his left leg
I give him a huge bite and taste the remnants, yummy

He flicks me off with a shake of his leg
But I'm tenacious and I jump back on his right leg
He's now wide awake and heading for the toilet
I dig my teeth and claws in to stop falling

Out of the toilet he goes to have breakfast
I gobble some more and enjoy my own breakfast
Next back to the bathroom and into the shower
So I jump off in haste and head back to the bedroom

He's off to work so I have to feed off dead skin
Until he returns in the evening when I will befriend him again
I wait in the bedroom until he arrives home and changes into
home clothes
I jump into the air and catch onto one of his sleeves

I manoeuvre and eventually latch onto his arm
I have my feast as he feasts on his dinner
Then he sits on the sofa to watch the football
And I jump around until I reach his upper back

He's off again to take another shower
So I leap off, flit from the carpet to the bedroom and onto his bed
My peripatetic nature keeping me fit, healthy and frisky
I wait on his pillow until he rests down at night

Once he starts snoring I begin my nocturnal banquet

My Little Pony

My little pony is like my little sister
Cantering through lush green pastures
Exploring the nooks and crannies
Roving through all the valleys, at all times of year

Searching for a stallion
Someone to give her heart to
Someone to love her truly
And make her feel special

Galloping across the meadows
Past hedgerows and grazing cattle
Always forgiving and forgetting
And trotting along with glee.

Narcissus

Looking at my reflection in the Aegean Sea
I see Hercules, Adonis and Achilles

Fictional self-imagery gives me freedom from reality
My ravishing handsomeness makes me feel mighty

Then one day Osiris whispered softly to me
And I pleaded with him for the key to eternal youth and
immortality

Alas I ended up standing over a stagnant pool
Loving myself now felt so cruel

Neighbours

Neighbours can be your saviour
So don't think its hard labour
To do them a favour

Out of love not necessity
Whatever the recipe
Just find the goodwill

You don't need any skill
Even if you are over the hill
Or crushed by bills

Neighbourliness tis bliss
Yes you will always be my guest
You and all the rest

As I go on life's quest
In my white cotton sleeveless vest
To make all the neighbourhoods brim
With neighbourliness zest

Neutrino

The infinite power of the infinitesimal

The intricate mechanisms of quantum mechanics

From m boson to quark

There's always an electric spark

Nigel

When life is all about the other half
And the self retreats to the inner citadel
You become the Orc and the Halfling
On your wife's mantelpiece

When all of your life revolves around marriage
And you discard David Deida's way
You'll forge a new path like a savage
But at least you did it your way

Nightmare

Awoken by a sudden jolt
The thought that gripped me by the throat
I saw a demon glaring down
I felt a dagger running down my spine

Sweat poured down my naked body
I felt the cold wooden floor beneath my feet
Each step was laboured and hard to complete
I felt like I was made of lead, each limb a deadweight

An eerie silence and a deafening hush
The still night air embraced every inch of my cold body
I twisted and turned to release the shackles
But the demon laughed and grinned with glee

I felt like a pawn in the demon's deadly game
A plaything in his sardonic game of chess
Hooded knights, rooks and bishops I faced
My only escape was to hoodwink and entrance them into thinking I was an illusion

Yama the lion roared and started its pursuit
It was the demon's pet and it smelt of Hades
I ran on hot coals until my feet were blistered
Until my lungs ached and my limbs gave up

I climbed a tree to hide from the beast

But it jumped and clawed viciously at me

I twisted and turned and kicked and punched

Until I awoke startled and confused in the emergency room

Night shift

Toiling away while the whole world is asleep
Are the night workers trying to earn their keep

It took a while for my body to get accustomed
To the night shift routine and its peculiar customs

I still found it hard to avoid the three am munchies
Of sausage rolls, chocolates and French cheese

I used to drink Red Bull aplenty
To keep me alert and ever so friendly

The early morning sun was the warning
That my shift was ending and the day was dawning

As commuters rushed to the tube station heading to work
I was heading home tired and wishing to be beamed up like
Captain Kirk

No reception

On New Years Eve trying to send out greetings

Throughout the flight and as the plane taxis, takes off and lands

In hospitals, on underground trains and certain railway carriages

In the remotest reaches of Borneo and Maccu Picchu

In parts of the country out of reach by the nearest transmission beacon

On a cold rainy wintry night in an unfamiliar place trying to call for assistance

Northern Line Ghost

Amelia's Paranormal Diary – 9 January 2013

As she sat on the southbound Northern line tube train on her way home at 11pm, Amelia felt uneasy, she looked around and saw one man on the far side of her carriage sitting with his head resting on one side sleeping. She looked closely and could see the slow rise and fall of his chest but something made her anxious, she felt she was being watched, initially she thought she was being paranoid, it was late at night and she usually felt nervous travelling on the tube at this time.

She shuffled in her seat a little before closing her eyes and attempting to get forty winks. Two minutes later as the train approached Balham station it suddenly screeched to a halt. She opened her eyes alarmed, she turned to her right and saw a man looking at her but it was no ordinary man, it was a ghost. Amelia was horrified and began gasping for breath. She tried to move but her body felt glued to her seat, she rubbed her eyes and looked again at the apparition, the man was not moving.

Amelia gradually got up from her seat; her legs felt like lead, she inched her way towards the carriage to her left which seemed to have a few passengers in it. Amelia didn't believe in ghosts, but what was about to happen made her question her beliefs in the paranormal. As she trudged along she turned back to see the ghost, it smiled at her before coming forward to introduce itself. "My name is Gunther" the ghost said slowly, his words slightly slurred, "I am stuck in a nether world between heaven and hell, my heart was broken once and I am forever confined to wandering these tube tunnels, every week at the same time, the same time that my heart was broken so many years ago." Amelia's heart melted and she felt sorrow for this strange heartbroken ghost, tears seared up inside as she looked at him and saw how eager he was for a response, "don't worry" she said softly, noticing how the ghost listened intently to each word she said as if she was speaking a foreign language.

Their conversation was interrupted by the train driver speaking through the tannoy speaker, "ladies and gentlemen, we apologise for the delay, we are being held at a red signal but we expect to be on the move shortly."

Gunther frowned and then said "I must go, can't keep all the passengers waiting." He turned and hobbled away before stepping through the closed tube door into the tunnel and his apparition slowly faded away…

Not in my name

Raw, raw, the law has a flaw

Thousands unite to one day see justice and fairness unfrozen and thaw

Shaken and rocked by an event that no-one foresaw

When fairness, equality and impartiality again evaporated from the law

Supreme Court justice led to injustice

The world was a witness

To the state execution of an innocent man without compassion or fairness

Revealing discrimination, prejudice and bigotry of a system that is heartless

New evidence made Troy's conviction unsafe and unclear

The appeal courts they did rehear

Yet justice did not appear

Now the courts we can no longer revere

Saw, saw, I saw all the tears

And all the fear

That fateful day in Georgia, when all did become queer

When justice did not appear

NOW

NOW is our only reality

NOW is the time to make it happen

Live in the present, know your past and hope for the future

The past will always be but a distant memory and the future an unseen dream

Obama

The time had come for a change
A break from an old divisive politics
A campaign with grit and vision
Promising hope to those who had none

A leader's role requires vision
When everyone else is a critic
A new beginning you have brought
A new and harmonious song

In the midst of policy
You see the human cost
In the midst of the red tape
You see the most in need

The real life inspector gadget
With a bag full of tricks
The new age magician
Trying to make the impossible possible

Ocean liner

Reminisce, slide back, relax and buy a ticket
Then check in and board the imaginary ocean liner

The voyage on the ocean of memories begins
Happy halcyon days play out on the liner's cinema screen

From port to starboard and as you look to the horizon
Memories flood by as the liner cruises along majestically

The ocean has captured days of yore
Your ancestors' dreams and tales galore

When the voyage ends your memories will be stored
So that future passengers will marvel at your amazing feats

Ode to Zephaniah

Speaking what's on your mind, poetically

Standing up for what you believe, fearlessly

Listening to the calls of the marginalised, poor, oppressed and victimised,

magnanimously

Speaking the unspeakable, for those without a voice, unquestionably

Living to make the world better, most definitely

Ogunshakin

The monster lurks in the deep

Chasing me through its unsolvable three dimensional maze like a wolf chasing a sheep

I toss and turn trying to break free from somnambulist clamour and escape the confines of Sauron's keep

But I am in exile in Mordor, too far from the safety of Helm's Deep

Shuttled unceremoniously without food, drink or sleep through the Dark Portal until Azeroth opens its door

I am enlisted forthwith by the Alliance to battle Garrosh's Hordes and banish them far from Theramore Isle's fair shores

Sensory overload and cranial overstimulation ensures until Deathwing the Destroyer's lava breath awakens from deep within my subconscious the sleeping half-human, half-yoma Claymore

Ogunshakin will be vanquished and legendary tales of the astounding and fortuitous victory will eventually slip into folklore

One small step for man

A little dot is what the Earth looks like from the Moon

The Apollo team took humankind to new heights and caused world celebration

But the most significant step for man has to come soon

When great advances gives kryptonite to the masses

Online dating

Let's all go and Face Party
Or join Friend Finders in search of the best Match
Plenty of Fish to Meet at Last
Love and Friends and all things nice

My Single Friend is such a Flirtbox
Eager for Loopy Love in the Kiss Café
Matching Pants should Be2gether
Urban Socials want to Be Naughty

Too love sick to enter Xfactor dating
Groovy Zoosk advises Trust Cupid
Play and flirt or Fast Flirting sounds enticing
But i try Cheekytflirt instead

Smooch and be2
Since I am free tonight
So I don't mind a Canoodle
Or the whole kit and caboodle

Girls date for free
Until two hearts meet
A Sugardaddy you may find
Who'll always be there for you

On a Midsummer's eve
Another chance of love beckons
So let nature take its course
Or go direct with Dating Direct

Am I hot or not?
Let the votes decide
Smart dating not Daydream dating
Just another day in the world of online dating

On loan

Endless searching for an out of print book

A trek to the local library to have a quick look

The online catalogue states the book is on the shelf

But hours later after much toiling the proclamation: the book is
on loan

It was the only book I needed for my unfinished thesis

So hard to find that it wasn't even on Amazon

Searching all London's libraries and booksellers without much
avail

Until one copy shows up in a library in St. John's Wood but
when I arrive I am told it is on loan!

On passing by

It all started with a look, a passing glance and a smile

I couldn't help but stare, your beauty beyond compare

I tripped and fell but tried to style it out

You stopped and turned, I smiled and commented on how amazingly stunning you looked

The initial talk was brief, I was hypnotised by your sexy eyes

The dainty and sultry way you walked, and the seductive way you talked

Not to mention all your curves, the eyes they did observe

I knew at that moment you were the one who will make me forget where I was and who I am; the one that will make time stand still

Each moment we shared you made me feel like I could walk on water

A love that rose like a volcano from the depths of the ocean

Creating an island paradise that others can now see and admire

Love can move mountains, conquer the unconquerable and make the impossible possible

On the terraces

Going back to days of yore

When football was about passion and love of the game

Not money, merchandising and satellite TV deals

The fan base is more global

As football's coverage spreads

It's more about the bottom line, revenues and share prices

They say the game has changed and gone more upmarket

I say it's priced out the real supporters

And gone off target

Opium

Poetry, the opium of the masses
Comes to thee from far yonder

Extemporizing in full flow
Like a river that has bursts its banks

Words surge in the overflow
Bringing silt, pebbles, and soil

To nourish all those willing to receive
And to give succour to all in need

Like manna from heaven
Like nectar from nature's bosom

Question not the source
Experience the inspiration coming alive through words

Fires burn inside with amazement
The message a treasure beyond pleasure

Listen to the message, exalt not the messenger
Lest the message be muddied and forgotten

Oprah

Oh queen of my television

Passing on knowledge to the masses
Raising awareness

And always trying to do good

Heaven will remember your kind heart

Parking

Counting down the time

To six thirty, when the church bells chime

At last it is the time

When it won't cost me a dime

I'm always filled with glee

When I avoid the exorbitant parking fee

Penthouse and Pavement (Heaven 17)

From the city of the seven hills
Of stainless steel, mines and mills

Came electric pop and iconic rock
Gatecrashing through with the projectable digital clock

From the sour pavement
To the saccharin penthouse

No artificial preservatives or additives added to the music
Just Yorkshire bitter and lots of glitter

People's Peers

The people peers, launched with such fanfare and cheer

Twas a chance for all to be represented in the lordships house

But what do we have, apart from the usual suspects

A lost opportunity to make the other place truly different

The vetting scheme doesn't make it clear it's not for the average Joe

It's for Joe the QC, the director or the professor, not Joe the bricklayer, plumber or bin man

Plato's Republic rather than representative democracy

Philosophers kings rather than Kevin and Perry

Permanence of Impermanence

Even though I am here, I am but a drop in the ocean
The permanence of impermanence can be stifling at times
So don't take yourself too seriously

In 2090 all that remains of me will be these words on this page
In history's great storybook, time is a relative notion

Phillipe Petit

No challenge too big
No barrier to life

Living in the sky where the air is thin
Gently gliding along like a swan on a lake

When every step could have been his last
Life on a tightrope is never dull

Photogenic

A picture can tell a story
Capturing me at dawn or dusk in my full glory
I look much better in person or so I've been told
Loving the camera lens since two years old

Today, my image is my brand
Just like Russell Brand
So I strive to look the best I can
And work on that golden tan

But appearances can be deceptive
Since airbrushing is now so creative
I try not to get upset by a bad photo
Or I'll end up going loco

Pizza

Margherita, Hawaiian or meat feast

Deep pan rather than thin crust

Extra toppings and more mozzarella

Garlic bread, potato wedges and coleslaw as a side order as well

Pizza always goes down a treat

Whether on my way home from work

Or when I'm watching a DVD on lazy Sundays

And especially for breakfast after a long night dancing and
drinking tequilas

Poem from the soul

Drops of dew glisten on the leaf
Deep in the forest of the night

Listen closely and you will hear
A poem from the soul

Portugal

I left my heart in Portugal

Now I sing the song of the madrigal

At night still reminiscing about the precious moments that captured my soul

The people, the beauty, the vibrancy, and the Portuguese passion of life which I cannot but extol

I left part of my soul in the pracas of Lisboa

Rossio, Belem, Cais do sodre and Alfama tattooed their images onto my eager retina

The blessed Sintra put me under its spell

Timeless riches so ubiquitous and mesmerising that the environ caused a spiritual groundswell

I left Cristo Rei by sending out a song of peace

That I hope travels further than Vasco da Gama; its melody never to cease

I sent out a prayer pinned to the wings of a hovering seagull

It flew up into the clear blue sky and then glided down and perched on an ocean liner's hull

I left a sandcastle dedicated to all poets in Cascais

May their poems enlighten the weary and brighten their bleakest days

For the soul of Portugal has whispered softly to me

And I now whisper back to you though these words from across the sea

Priya the Rollercoaster

You take me high, you take me low
Which ever way we go, we went with the flow

While it lasted, we had a blast
Without any past, we just connected so fast

You blindfolded me and made me march
On a cold winters day near Marble Arch

Probability

What are the chances of winning the Euromillions jackpot?
Probably more chance of turning into a crackpot

What are the chances of becoming Prime Minister?
Probably more chance of becoming a church minister

What are the chances of travelling to Mars?
Probably more chance of becoming a local government tsar

What are the chances of becoming a Formula One racing driver?
Probably more chance of becoming a deep sea diver

What are the chances of becoming a champion heavyweight fighter?
Probably more chance of becoming an acclaimed writer

Living life.
Playing the odds.

Psychosomatic

Autonomous automation in the engine room of the soul

Visceral urges spreading beyond bounds

Vicissitudes of the spirit invokes the whole

Quintessential yearnings drive the corporal machine into the impound

Melodramatic cravings that languish slowly push the body out of control

Unquenchable appetites and hungers not kept within sound grounds

Claustrophobic conditions engages the anatomy's flight or fight metabolism

Unable to switch off from the triggers before the next knockdown

Excessive stress activates the body's red light mechanism

Still powerless to engage with the soul and go to the hole for a six point touchdown

Metamorphosis from psychosis the only propitious resolution

Or the prognosis is break down, melt down and eventually shut down

Rage

Feel the rage, feel the fury
I am a human, glued to the electric chair

A cage of emotions slowly ripping limb from limb
A vernal uprising, the October revolution

Chimerical provender feeding the hovel's captives
Bereft and forlorn, no longer pugnacious and puissant

Pitching bacchanalia against piousness
Pacify, sublimate and meditate

Pouring down from the empyrean
The synesthetic overload failing to assuage as the blood simmers
and boils

Life is an aleatorial adventure
So never be supercilious

Don't look to Semiotics
Or you may end up senescent and manacled

Don't look to logical positivism
Words are not enough

Don't look for denouement
There is none

Feel the rage, feel the fury
I am a human, glued to the electric chair

Reincarnation

The cradle so peaceful and still
Watched over and guarded by loving parents
So little is remembered of this wondrous time
When all the world flashes past in a haze

The first little steps and the first words are spoken
Something new inside has just awoken
Learning brings a whole new dimension
As limbs grow stronger and the world is set in motion

The kindergarten years a joy to behold
Glimpse of the wider world await
Then primary school and more independence
A sense of self and who I am

Learning about oneself through social interaction
The primary school playground is my whole world
Friendships, rivalries and close bonds are formed
A microcosm of the world at large

The teenage trip so hard at first
At times I am shy, then aggressive and other times nonchalant
Searching for identity and learning more of oneself
The hormones rage and the mind goes wild

A time to experiment and a time to live
Strangled by rules its times to break free
Live for today and think not of the future
Since twenty one seems like an eternity away

The age of youth so vibrant and full
A voyage of discovery and self reflection
Not a care in the world and all my life ahead
Impossible is nothing so I try to make it real

Thirties set in and family commences
The joys, thrills and spills of parenthood
Responsibility of being a good role model to my offspring
A new role, a new position in self and world

Fifties and more seniority and respect is commanded
I have my views which are borne through toil and experience
A time to look forward to the fruits of my labour
A new journey begins as the shell of my body transforms

Finally old age and the last reincarnation is complete
Prior to the moribund shell that I will one day become
A time to reflect and pass on wise anecdotes
A tradition of storytelling and nurturing younglings

Each stage of life is a new reincarnation
A bodily transformation that always amazes

The mind also transforms throughout each phase

The perfect circle of life progresses as each stage enraptures

Riding lady luck

Riding lady luck and you take your chance

But just like the casino, the odds always favour the house

So play dice with life and you may come up trumps

Or the river card may send you home in tatters and cramps

Riding lady luck in the game of love

Too many fish in the sea and love seems like a fun game

Things will change with time and tide

Settle down before you end up all alone and with no one to confide

Riding lady luck because you're young, fit and carefree

In your twenties now and still all to play for

Hit your forties and it's time for stability and cautiousness

Or you'll find yourself out of bounds and with no way back

Riding lady luck in the gambling game

It's a thrill with no spills and it can be a nice little earner

But at the end of the day, lady luck is looking on from overhead

Like a Janus faced sceptre, the next number may be yours

Riot

In the midst of the city's maelstrom

The internal flame smoulders

The calm before the storm

The laughter and the chatterbox's incessant bickering

Provoking internal self-combustion

And a constant unnerving rustling

A healthy and fulfilling lifestyle

Is not possible

For those on the destitute diet

Constant hustling for work

And living hand to mouth

One day the dispossessed will switch to all out riot

RNLI

In severe gale force winds and through the roughest seas

Brave lifeboat crews battle to save a stricken cargo ship

The icy cold sea waters battering boat and crew like a lion
tamer's whip

Then the visibility worsens as the storm draws in

Undeterred the experienced coxswain courageously attempts the
rescue and bring the crew safely in

Another night and the call comes in at half past one

A crew in distress

Their submerged yacht now lifeless

Out to sea as quick as can be

RNLI to the rescue, the gods of the sea

Rodin's thinker

Still and serene

So calm on the surface

The outer fascade

The superficial papier-mâché

Take the trouble to look beyond the epidermis

And the placid surface of the lake

Then the outstanding beauty that lies close to the ocean's sea bed
will be discovered

The coral reefs and blossoming marine wildlife will reveal itself

The philosophies of Socrates

The machinations of Machiavelli

The teachings of Buddha

The propagations of The Federalist Papers

The brain in thought

Computing all of life's conundrums

Pondering the unanswerable mysteries of life

Is a wonderful awe-inspiring sight

Roma

Oh charisma, history, sunshine and beauty

Lying on the banks of the Tiber, eating pizza and drinking fine wine

Oh romance, fortitude, fuoco and Forza

Relaxing outside Il Colosseo, thinking of gladiatorial games and imperial might

Oh splendour, paramour, enchantment and eternal flame

Standing and surveying Roma the from atop of the Basilica San Pietro

Routemaster

It started with an idea

Then it became a concept

After that it turned into a prototype

Before finally it hit the streets of the capital

The Idea:

Modernizing without metamorphosis

The best of the old mixed with the new

Greener but still painted red

More passengers, more efficiency, better designed

The Concept:

Three doors instead of two

Two staircases instead of one

[And optional conductor]

Route N155

Waiting at the bus stop near to Trafalgar Square

Just like in days of yore when I was a student filled with overflowing gusto and flair

Hoping for seat but wanting to avoid the upper deck

Where drunken louts slumber and snore after clubbing and partying in central London

Keeping a low profile unless travelling back with friends

Listening to the stories, escapades and experiences of fellow N155 travellers

The bus twists and turns through the desolate streets of south London

And slowly churns out tired revellers and night workers into the frosty night sky

Running On Empty

The glass is half full
The glass is half empty
There is something missing inside

I've been around the block
Too many times to clock
Nietzche told me there was something empty inside

I've searched the depths of all souls
For the missing part to make it whole
Wondering if there is something missing inside

I've sat at night gazing at the sun, moon and stars
A solitary mortal on the banks of the River Ganges
To find that there is nothing missing inside

Saudade

I sit and think and think and think
Even more abstruse than Rodin's Thinker

I am an empty vessel that cannot be filled
Drunk by the sound of seraphs serenading Diana from Mount
Olympus' mighty hill

I sing a song of oblation
Until my soul reaches a state of extreme repletion

Time and tide doth wait for no man
Marathon runners revamp on the Pilgrim's van

Precious drop in the seventy billion ocean
Davy Jones's locker is always in motion

Scented roses

Roses are red

Tulips are orange

The grass is green

Daffodils are yellow

Daises are white

Lilies are fawn

The sky is blue

The Ewya tree is Technicolor
Technicolor

My love is red

My work is orange

My world is green

My car is yellow

My house is white

My dreams are fawn

My jeans are blue

My life is lived in

Scotland to Surrey by night

And what a journey it shall be
Leaving Glasgow once a month late at night
Venturing via the M8, M74, M6, M42, M40 and finally M25
Through wind and rain I've travelled on
Turning down the windows to get some fresh air
To stop me from drifting across sleep's frontier
The unlit motorway twists and turns
Like the tail of a scorpion
Or the writhing of a python that's ready to pounce

Turning up the volume of my car stereo
To keep sleep's welcoming bosom from drawing me closer
The beats are pounding
Just like my ears
An audience of one
Just me and the silent night
Not another car on the motorway for company
The pumping music carries across the night sky
Brahms, Bryan Adams, Lady Gaga, Kesha and N-Dubz

An orchestra on wheels travelling at seventy miles an hour
Pushing away the luring hand of sleep
Until glimpses of brightness appear on the horizon
The first rays of sun break through night's shadow
And the sky gradually brightens

As the body lightens
And the senses once again heighten
The early morning sun shakes the body alive
Free from the night's tight clasp

The stomach now begins to call for a breaking of the night fast
The motorway services provide an essential respite
To replenish lost energy and get forty winks
Then onwards again towards the final stretch
Exhausted and dreaming only of my welcoming divan bed
Confronted by commuters on their way to work
More tests of patience and concentration to endure
Until final destination
And I slip into the wide open arms of sleep

Second Life

A flickr of light here and lunar storm there
From utopia to Nextopia
Cupid will pluck you from your present life
Giving you a Second Life that's is less synthetic

In Second Life
I can live twice
This time exactly as I desire
So I become James Bond

Maybe I will stick with life as a Second Life avatar
Because I'm so popular and powerful
And I can make happiness fall like rain in a monsoon
Whereas real life can be so dull and dreary if there is no boon

No sooner than I think of this
Than an esteemed Second Life friend approaches
"Hello my friend, how art thou" I say
"Glad tidings or rage ye seek?"

He replied "I'm a peaceful fellow, just very mellow
Forgive me if I seem a tad shallow
Verily I say, I'm your friend for today
But tomorrow alas I can't vouch safe

For we never will know

Where we'll be in an hour

And tomorrow is a lifetime away"

And then he turned to go on his way

Self-Portrait

What do I see when looking in the mirror?

A face that changes as the years roll by

But what is it about this face that I always see?

Is it only the outer coating of the soul housed within?

Do we see ourselves according to how the media says we should look?

Or do we view our image according to our own bespoke paradigm?

Self-image, self-reflection, self-portrait and increasingly self-obsession

An unhealthy lifelong Narcissistic solipsism now infecting children as young as seven

If it is true that beauty is only skin deep

Then why do we take so long plucking, pruning and styling?

Our face and its multitude of expressions are but the window to the soul

When we next look at ourselves in the mirror, can we see beyond the surface?

Self-Service

Taylorist foundations and Fordist proclamations
A new generation of technological invention

Instead of being served, it's now self-service
Automated trams, telephone and banking services

No more human operated
It's now computer generated

Artificial intelligence
Only tests an artist's patience

For better or worse
Soon there will be robots writing verse

Sensory perception

In the pitch black night I couldn't see
The Moon and stars were hidden by cloud
My auditory system took the strain
And suddenly I could hear like never before

Blindfolded for fun to play the Vino game
I sampled wines from around the world
Setting on a new world red
My gustatory system loving the banquet

Sampling eau de toilette at the boutique
My olfactory system put to the test
Sweet top notes of juniper berry and wild flowers
And invigorating and seductive middle and base notes

A night of passion on the beach
Kinaesthetic senses accentuated like never before
When the primary visual machinery has a rest
New heights of sensory perception can be reached

Seven Seas

Cod Liver Oil is lodged in the top cupboard
Above the melee of kitchen accoutrements

A clear yellow golden hue
A subtle mellow syrupy broth

Shallow graves

The shallow grave of the unknown lies unattended

The heather grows and the knotweed encircles

Leaving a space that looks similar to any other in the vicinity

So that no one would ever know that someone was buried there

The shallow graves of the earthquake, tsunami and flood victims protrude

Transmogrifying the landscape and marking the place forever in local folklore

Another emblem of nature's furious power

Scarring local communities and leaving the survivors crestfallen

The shallow graves of those massacred in civil wars and ethnic cleansing

Another reminder of humankind's inability to get along, humankind's inhumanity to other humans and humankind's capacity for evil

Causing intergenerational angst and leaving generations swearing revenge and retribution

The saga between Juno and Aeneas shall replay again

Shoot to goal

"Where's the grit, where's the belief, when you step out there
you give your heart"
"I hear you boss, will do that aye"

"Go on Stevie, make it true"
"aiiight there mate, let us concentrate"

"David, slow and steady ok?"
"hear you gov, will keep the pace"

"Michael, get a move on son"
"Will do so but me leg ain't got over that cramp yet"

"You want this free kick Ryan, let us know?"
"Aye, mine it is, just give us cover"

"Bend it right o'er the wall"
"No worries fella, gonna belt it clean"

"Quick Frank, pass it ere"
"I'll switch with you, pass through the middle"

"Fernando, you want to take the penalty we've just been
awarded?"
"I'll take it boss, I'm ready to go"

"Lads, it's going into overtime so keep your strength"
"Pass us that drink; I'm in need of some"

"Keep it tight and they'll go offside"
"All pull up when Kaka runs"

"Is it me they wanna sub?"
"Yeah mate you are off, you're sub'd again"

"Five minutes now and victory will be ours"
"Hold the line, damn here they come again"

"One final push we mustn't lose"
"Get everyone up and shoot to goal"

Silverknowles

I walked down the narrow winding road leading to the Silverknowles Promenade area, I could see Cramond Island in the distance and as I got closer to the promenade, I could smell the freshness of the sea, hear and see the seagulls hovering above, and almost taste the fresh and slightly salty sea air in my mouth.

As I reached the main promenade walkway, I looked out at the island and into the vast ocean, it was so breathtaking, The Sun was shining brightly and the sea gulls dipped down towards the ocean's surface before rising again. I slowly went down the stone stairwell leading to the rocky beach area and chose a comfy rock to sit on. Being much lower than the walkway and so close to the sea made it an almost different experience, like I had reached a place of tranquillity and oneness with nature and at the same time I could feel the power of the ocean and its vast almost limitless reach. As I sat there, I felt so in tune with the ocean's movements.

The ocean looked so serene, the ocean current glided ever so gently along. Yet when I looked nearer to the shore I saw the waves pounding the shore, each wave riding the crest of the previous one. I then began to realise how powerful the ocean was and the immense strength that lies within its depths. I listened to the sound of the waves pounding the sea shore over and over again, and watched the wisp of the white surf as each wave lashed upon the open shore.

Silver surfer

Living the life of a sexagenarian is still all thrills and spills
Settled in life and full of bravado

As a septuagenarian time has started to take its toil
Not the spritely chicken I once was when I was twenty one

As an octogenarian I love seeing my grandchildren
Telling them stories and fables of times of yore

I survived to be a nonagenarian so I can't really complain
I've seen so many wars, scientific inventions, technological
changes and space explorations

Six pomegranate seeds

Eaten by Proserpine when taken by Pluto to the Underworld
Now six months of the year harvests fail and there is drought
As Ceres mourns the fate of her daughter
The pity of Jupiter and Juno is not enough to constrain
Man's consternation at the God's lack of remedial action

Sleep

I lie awake and count the sheep
I've run the New York marathon three times already in my sleep

Another all night party that pushed back sleep
The next day's afternoon lecture when I fell asleep

Mediterranean siestas I seem to favour
Getting rejuvenating afternoon kip is something I still savour

The early evening nap I've been told is best to avoid
An old wives tale that all parents have deployed

Too hard to control this insatiable beast's nerve
Only learn to give it the respect it deserves

Snow

Snow inches thick wherever I look
Icy snow and grit spewed across the road

Icicles hanging from the greenhouse ceiling
The Arctic is calling and delivering its welcome message

Time seems to stand still as picture postcard scenes come alive
The landscape transformed into picturesque splendour

Hidden from view the fox hole and the rabbit burrow
Now under a blanket of snow, oblivious to the rain and pending morrow

City workers trundle along slip sliding across the icy patches
Children make snowmen and teenagers make snowballs that they eagerly dispatch

Soldier

Soldier from the start

Soldier in the morning

Soldier in the evening

Soldier at the convent

Soldier at work

Soldier as a daughter

Soldier as a wife

Soldier as a mother

Soldier as a sister

Soldier in the good times

Soldier in the bad times

Soldier to strangers

Soldier to the people

Soldier to the last

Soldiering through adversity

Soldiering through the pain

Soldiering with a smile.

Solitude

On my own in this grand universe, lying on a white sandy beach and looking at the full Moon above

The vast ocean ahead is so calm and so powerful, each wave now breaking a little further up the shoreline

It is 11 pm at night and a cold wind blows, a cat meows in the distance and the wind whispers in the trees

All alone to savour this beauty; nature and the universe at peace and at sleep

Sonatina No.1 in G

Just me and my piano

Tickling the ivories is enough to take me away
To a place of serenity
To the surface of the Moon

I get lost as I play Beethoven's masterpiece
Sonatina No.1 in G

My body sways with the subtle change in pitch and cadence
My soul ignites and dances carefree

Son et lumière

The Sun has burst its banks

I can hear Tchaikovsky's Nutcracker Suite carried inland by the wind

The night air jolts alive with the recorded voices of historic visionaries

Replete with burgeoning multicoloured balloons and dazzling lighting

A spectacle that even the Delphic oracle couldn't foresee

History alive and buzzing to the sound of rhythm and blues

Sonnet 2010.2

Tis is the love of my life and for all eternity

My heart beats longingly and I throw caution to the wind

From far and wide I travel to declare my desire and longing

The flame burns brighter each time I hear her sweet voice

Each time she smiles at me time stands still and my heart skips a beat

Angel in the night that makes the heart glow in a fiery frenzy

Volcanic larvae flurries across field and meadow until reaching the placid ocean

Lighting the ocean with waves of rapacious lasciviousness

Until a tsunami of love engulfs the entire globe

And the universe hears the raucous calls of the suitors

Cupid's arrow hits the mark and my beloved and I are united

Love so pure and gentle that the stars twinkle gleefully

Two songbirds merrily singing in the sun, rain and snow

Until we grow old and tell stories by the fire

Sonnet 2010.3

Journey of the magi through the desert storm and unforgiving heat

Journey of the lovers searching for their one true love

Journey full of pitfalls, quakes and setbacks but success will eventually come

Journeying far and wide with many peaks and troughs

Journeying high and low in hope but not in vain

Journeying near and far through fog, blizzards and hurricanes

Journeying itself driven by the locomotive of the heart

Journeying alone for the one to call your own

Journeying across continents, time zones and terrains

Journeying never ceases however fraught the journey is

Journeying to the centre of the Earth to reach the inner core

Journeying past the point of no return to reach the chosen land

Finally arriving at the place you longed desperately to be

Finally in the arms of your beloved and living happily ever after

Sonnet 2010.4

To love and be loved tis all one doth wish

Just like teenage love that knows no limits, that never says never

Far from the vagaries of predilection and aesthetics

You are my rock of protection and my shining light

Raw passion and romance

Raw emotion and desire

No mountain too high

Nothing to quench this lustful inculcation

Lying awake together on the beach looking up at the Moon and the stars

An infinite honeymoon

An everlasting romance

Let the wild thoughts race

Set the emotions apace

Tis not a moment to waste!

South London's finest

Take the high road
Or take the Lowe road

A path less trodden
Is the way of the visionary

A gait that's your trait
Never a meagre trot since you left the cot

Plaudits and kudos keep mounting
So many already but you keep on crafting and grafting

Treading the sidewalks and byways with a purpose
Never trespassing outside your moral compass

South London's finest
London's wisest and brightest

Sparks fly on the dance floor

Six thirty the church bell chimes
Another evening approaches fast and you're feeling fine
The street lights stutter on and then shine

A crisp cool breeze signals the entrance of the night
Clubbers and partygoers getting ready to look out of sight
The dance floor looks set to ignite

Heading to the venue dancing and singing
Happy vibes in full swing
Friends greeting each other with warm embraces, happy faces
and car music pumping

Mesmerized by the dancing neon lights
A tingle down the spine as you enter the spotlight
Your moves are tight; you set the dance floor alight

It's time to leave the world outside
And let sparks fly on the dance floor
This is your night, just you and the dance floor

Spider

Spider, Spider, up there so sly

Hark, Hark, what does thou see there

Hiding, Hiding in the dark

Crawling, Crawling into creeks

Spinning, Spinning all those webs

Trapping, Trapping creatures in your spell

Running, Running when caught in the glare

Spider, Spider, you are so sly

Spiritual loving

When love moves beyond physical pleasure

And two souls become one

Physical union then becomes a heavenly meeting

A perfect unison of spiritual loving

Of body, mind and soul as one

Stag party

A few pints and the day is off to a raucous beginning

A ride on the clipper playing 'name that tune' leaves all the party singing

A powerboat trip down the Thames whets the appetite

It's early afternoon now and the party basks in the glorious sunlight

Go karting is a buzz but twists and turns leave the neck a little strained

Joe is the winner so he shouts and screams and is hard to constrain

An evening rendezvous at an exclusive restaurant kicks the evening into full swing

Exotic food, sumptuous dessert and Persian belly-dancers leave the eyes and other unnamed parts of some of the party bulging

An unplanned stop at a burlesque club gets the stags hot under the collar

Too much indulgence and the seductress leaves the stags panting and quickly running out of dollars

Last night of freedom before jumping on the horse and carriage

Living solo was fun but too much like living in the jungle so it's time to get ready to be tied to the reigns of marriage

Summer Mayhem

Looking for the mire
I can see the desire
The rioters, looters and arsonists
Filled with passion and a belly full of fire

CCTV captures the moments of social visceral expurgation
Mayhem rules instead of the rule of law
Shops close early and businesses shut
When summer mayhem rules the roost

Sun Tzu's maze

I'm tired of the mendacity, Chutzpah, sardonic and obstreperous vitriolic invectives

I'm tired of the knavery, chicanery, cantankerousness, fastidiousness and furtive machinations

I will conjure up a coruscate philtre and inveigle you with quixotic charm and ebullient repartee

You say you love me now but in my heart I wonder

Will you still love me tomorrow?

Sweet tooth

Sweet tooth will eventually get what the sweet tooth wants
No matter the cost or the endless jaunts

Sudden cravings and late night supermarkets runs
Living at the mercy of the sweet tooth is not much fun

I will stop being dragged and being led
When the insatiable sweet tooth is finally fed

Tao

May the force be with you
Strong and weak will pull you
Electromagnetism will stun you
Gravity will drain you

The dance of protons and neutrons
Accompanied by encircling electrons
The cosmic dynamo
Formless, shapeless and incorporeal

Learn to adapt to the flow
Be the reed, not the oak tree
Change is life, said Heraclitus
Life is change, for better or worse

Talk Adolf radio

Tune in for machinations and subterfuge

Field plans being drawn up late at night that are more complex than a Rubik's cube

Only Bletchley can get close enough to the wall to decipher the talk Adolf cipher

Astonishing and fantastical pronouncements by a megalomaniac lifer

Broadcasting hedonistic laced shibboleths and fuelling iconoclastic beliefs

Until the Reich self combusts and chokes on broken teeth

Texting - the new lingua franca

Hi m8, u ok? Soz was l8, nt feelin gr8 :-(

2moz 7pm wud b gd, even gt u surprise lol ;-)

Lemme no asap, mtg nik l8r, tc :-)

The Abbey

The silence penetrates the soul

The power of spiritual union penetrate each pore

The deafening echo of peace and tranquillity

A collective journey and a path travelled in solitude

The liturgy, Eucharist and communion

A closeness with God and one's inner soul

The immense power, magnificence and love

To know Him, to know the Father, is to know You too

The glory of god reflected in the image of man

Wondrous celebration as you proclaim the Mysteries of the Rosary

Omnipresent and offering endless love to all who seek

You shall receive the strength you require when you need it most

No matter how many times you stumble, if you humbly seek

He will deliver you, He will comfort you

You will find salvation, peace and harmony

Rest easy and hold your head up high for He has not forsaken you

Though times may be tough and you shed a tear or two

Fear not, He walks with you through thick and thin

Look forward too, with hearts filled with joy

One day reunited with Him in heaven above!

The Albany

I sit outside on inviting chairs
Staring at Hampton Court Palace from a Thames-side lair
Majestic, captivating and alluring
Wolsey's palace still looks immaculate and endearing

The Thames ever still, tranquil and silent
I smile as the sun warms my body as I lie recumbant
Ducks waddle towards me in an orderly fashion
Looking for a modicum of food or any edible ration

The air grips tight and moisture clings close
Warmth that Cyprus has in a regular dose
As evening draws in the temperature drops
And mosquitoes emerge looking to feed until they drop

Time for a beer to wash down the food
And goad us all into a more raucous mood
The last bell rings so a final round is in order
Loud guffaws ring out as the banter gets louder

The Apprentice

<u>Initial:</u>

Thousand of applications received already so it won't be easy to get shortlisted

But a chance of fame and a hundred thousand pounds a year salary awaits

A twelve week job interview to test you to your limits

Your resume is not as important as your daily performance

Be personable, build alliances and fight tooth and nail in the boardroom

Whatever happens this will be an experience that will change your life

<u>Task One:</u>

The task may be beyond you and not your forte but you give it all you have

You've decided to be project leader and you plan a good strategy

There is too much to do and not enough time

So you delegate, prioritise, organise and initiate

You position your stall well, motivate your team and sell better than your opponents

You sleep well that night as another contestant is fired

<u>Task Four:</u>

You've made it this far and made some good friends

You're impressed with Sir Alan and his business acumen

But you've lost the ad campaign and you're called into the boardroom

You're fighting for survival since you didn't make the ad modern and stylish

You're criticised by the project leader and your life skills are called into question

But you survive the task knowing you need to up your game

Task Eight:

It's nearly the end, you see the finishing line ahead

You've been selected as project leader so it's all down to you

It's time for negotiation, leadership, strategic thinking and careful planning

You select two innovative products and the sales pitch goes well

But when the numbers are in, your opponents win and you return to the boardroom

The grilling is tougher, your fellow competitors are fiercer and you hear the two words you were wishing you didn't, "you're fired!"

The Charioteer

A comet left a stream of dust

Far above the Earth and deep in outer space

The naked eye searched the darkest night

For the charioteer riding across the universe in his golden chariot

Night after night the patient pilgrim searched the heavens

He watched the stars sparkle and the Moon wax and wane

He felt emboldened on nights when the full Moon illuminated his flowering garden of Eden

Evergreen in his solitude, there is fortitude and joy in his heart

One summer's night there was what looked like an asteroid in the sky

It was the charioteer riding on high

Traversing the universe

And now passing the Earth

The pilgrim smiled and raised his arms aloft

His body radiated white light and emitted iridescent embers

A thunderbolt raced down from the heavens and touched the pilgrim

And the pilgrim left the Earth and journeyed onwards in the heavens with the charioteer

The dusk chorus

The dusk slowly spreads it tentacles

Pushing the last rays of sun away once more

And darkness falls across the land

The blackbird begins the dusk chorus

The skylark joins in the symphony

A tweet here, a chirp there

The robin and chaffinch play lawn tennis

Just another instance of the daily trills and spills of wild birds at play

A spectacular crepuscular spectator sport

The Elusive Muse

The clocks ticks on
One, two and three am

Looking for inspiration
Ending up with perspiration

Searching for traction
Nocturnal trepidation

The body restless
The mind listless

Trying to write the next stanza
But I feel like a lifer pigeonholed in a 6 by 4 cell waiting for the bell to toll

No release comes
Sleep tugs at my sleeve and tries to get me to let go and drift away

I know the Elusive Muse is out there
So I don the mantle of Mulder and start searching

With psychic and telepathic communications
I try to summon her unsuccessfully

The daughters of Zeus and Mnemosyne
So mutable and ephemeral

I'm dressed and ready to go
I've accepted the mission to find the Elusive Muse but it will self destruct in one week

Undeterred I soldier on
I charter Air Force One

I venture from London to Paris
Then to Berlin, Warsaw and Rome

Onwards to Dubai, Delhi and Hong Kong
Then to Tokyo, Kuala Lumpur and Sydney

I see a rainbow in Sydney Harbour
I think I've found the precious elixir

I grab my laptop and start to type
I feel something deep and meaningful inside me

Alas it was a mirage, another false positive
Caused by an unacceptably rapid ingestion of copious amounts of milk chocolate

Back to the drawing board and time to call Scully

But she can't help; she's in London and fast asleep

With seventy two hours before the week is up

I find myself unable to eat, drink or sleep

In my hotel room I see ghosts of past laureates

They whisper sweet nothings and dance in the air, lack of sleep
and no food or drink has made me go mad

Now on the plane to San Francisco

I feel hopeful that I will find her there

On the flight I listen to a passenger next to me narrate her whole
life story

And her lifelong love for animals

Veterinary science is fascinating

But I'm a bit preoccupied so I just nod politely

I catch forty winks before the plane touches down at San
Francisco International

Suddenly I am rudely awoken by cabin crew asking me to return
my chair to the upright position

I am battling sleep's welcoming invitation

And my circadian rhythm's disruption from time zone
transgressions

The stewardess smiles

I can see sympathy in her face as she sees how dishevelled I have become

I smile back meekly

And focus again on the mission I have undertaken

Travelling along the Golden Gate Bridge again brings me no closer

So onwards to New York and the buzz of Manhattan

Straight to the top of the Empire State Building

And I'm feeling quite heady

I've been to the top a few times before

But never as a FBI Special Agent

An hour passes and I start to feel a chill

So I venture to Columbus Circle and feed my caffeine addiction

Only one place to go on this whistle-stop tour

Will Havana be the sanctuary of the philosopher's stone?

The heat comes as a welcome surprise as I leave Jose Marti International Airport

I go straight to old Havana

I relax in the Plaza de la Catedral

And look up at the magnificent Catedral de San Christobal de La Habana

Maybe what I am searching for is to be found in the house of god?

After two hour's reflection and some deep soul searching

I grab my laptop and start to type

Alas it was a chimera, just another delusion

I still have written not one single line

I return to my hotel room needing a lifeline

The plane heads over the English Channel and I pass back onto home soil

The captain announces that the plane is about to land at Heathrow

My mission is a failure

I give up the guise of Mulder

One week later on a lazy Sunday afternoon

I sit down and begin recounting my tale

Suddenly I feel a jolt from above

The inspiration that I traversed the globe for has entered me

It was inside me all along
Just hidden away

I searched far and wide
But never within

When I looked within I found the key to the treasure trove
I found the beautiful mystical Elusive Muse

The end of the weekend

The weekend draws to a close

I wish it was Friday night once again

So I can be changing into my party clothes instead of my nightclothes

And looking forward to a wild night with Stimpy and Ren

I'd like a four day week instead of the usual five

More time with my friends and more time with my family

So I wait until the next bank holiday arrives

And arrange a wacky excursion that's fandabidozi and lively

The far side of the Moon

It's 2 am and the mist clears from the hazy night sky

I'm looking up at the sky

Looking for inspiration

Searching for answers

Now it's 4.30 am and a chill has filled the early morning air

The Moon suddenly appears to come alive. It displays a luminous face and speaks with a Willo the Wisp voice

It whispers to me and suddenly Ka-Boom!

I end up with more rhetorical questions and open-ended three dimensional answers

The Fifth Element

Aether, quintessential element of the universe

Pure, perfect and existing throughout eternity

A molecule of the river of eternity

It survives the physical disintegration of the earthly body

Returning to the cosmic essence of pure spirit and energy

There's a heavenly presence inside all humans

Hidden far away from view

Many are unaware that the fifth element exists

And many let the fifth element dwindle

Not knowing it is accessible through meditation, prayer and spiritual reflection

The final rep

You've struggled hard, you've done nine sets
One set to go and then you've finished

It's the final hurdle but your body is shaky
The sweat pours down and the adrenaline races

You feel so pumped but your grip gives out
You close your eyes to focus and compose

The weight goes up and you scream out loud
You lower it down with an almighty puff

It's looking tough but each sinew is strained
Pushing yourself beyond the pain barrier is not an easy feat

Your raise the weight with an even greater roar
The weight is in the air but your body starts to tingle

You try to control the bar as you manoeuvre it down
But it hits the safety bars with a gigantic clang

Now to the final rep of the set and again you close your eyes
Summoning what strength and grit your tired body can muster

It's time to go, no time to waste

You let out a shriek as you summon all your raw animalistic powers

Your lift the bar, it's now halfway up
You close you eyes and cry out loud

You won't let the weight defeat you now
It's almost up, just inches to go

You heave and squeeze and finally it's there
You've won the primeval battle with the unforgiving weight

The joy of going for that final rep
A battle between body, mind and the weight

In gyms worldwide the battle ensues
Either the weight beats you or you conquer the weight

The fog of war

In the midst of the raging battle

Collateral damage and top secret kamikaze missions, extrajudicial killings and maniacal interrogations

Extraordinary rendition, black ops and twin-track policies

The fog of war engulfs, blinds, contaminates and spreads

But when the fog of war clears and the dust finally settles

And when the truth comes out and the victims emerge

Can you show you held to your principles and values?

Can you show you acted with courage and integrity even in the face of extraordinary adversity and unforgiving adversaries?

The Gemini mind, body and spirit

Split personality
Dual character

The way to his heart
Is through the intellect

Challenge and innovate
Or he'll leave you for new more interesting encounters

He loves to have more on his desk and on his plate
Than he can manage or digest

He has the gift of the gab
So can talk all night long

He's a wacky air sign
But ruled by mercurial steel

The extrovert and friendly socialite
Guaranteed to excite

The girls

Krystal, Aria, Lucy, Tiffany and Candy, you turn television into an intoxicating realm of naughty delight

How many hearts have you set alight?

The digital age has brought you closer to home

In living rooms, bedrooms and hotel rooms; you now have freedom to roam

Girlfriends don't understand their boyfriends infatuation

With your hypnotic smiles, provocative poses and entrancing gyrations

The savannah principle says the human brain can't comprehend twentieth century technological duality

The mirage of celluloid fantasy instead feeling like actual reality

But for many men around the globe tonight

You'll be taking them on a fantasy ride in the pale moonlight

The gladiatorial arena

Brave souls prepare before ye enter the arena of gladiator

Timed ye must not be, fight like an enraged and hungry alligator

Wear your heart on your sleeve and it will be crushed

Only the strong and brave will prosper here the rest will be
hushed

Perseverance, desire, belief and grit is needed to avoid defeat

Great and noble gifts await those who neither flinch nor retreat

Buckle up and enjoy the ride as you fight for your life

The prize is surely worth the strife

The great one

A yogic mind and sannyasin soul

Preaching goodwill and peace to the world without any personal goal

From one motherland to the next like a universal spirit

In the company of colleagues, family and friends, he is the eternal pundit

Always trying to do the best in a world full of subterfuge and complexity

Ever the simple person soldiering on without too much ado or corporeal property

The hitman

A shadow emerges out of the dark night
Dressed all in black and avoiding the street light

Vernal, insouciant and puissant like Agent 47
Suave and debonair like 007

He melts into the surroundings like a chameleon
He works professionally, clinically and methodically like Léon

A clean kill
The only thing that fits the bill

Then disappearing without a trace
Nobody getting a glimpse of his face

The Islands

The Sun shimmers and dances on the Skydome

The fresh breeze enlivens the soul

The white sands comforts the loins

The Islands are a treasure that has brought immense pleasure

Aquatic life blooms in the Islands' lagoons,

Birds, mammals, reptiles and wildflowers all thrive in unique natural habitats

A timeless sanctuary, full of unspoilt beauty

The Islands possess a spirit that inspires and invigorates

Taking the last ferry going back to the mainland

A mysterious stranger dressed all in black approaches and recounts

How residents of Ward Island struggled long and hard to remain there

An unforgettable conversation on an almost empty ferry gazing at the always enchanting Toronto skyline

Can life be as sweet as this moment is?

Or is this just a perfect memory that sadly will fade?

Can every moment be so inspiring, uplifting and pure?

Or will I end up reminiscing and recanting the beauty and oneness with the universe I felt here?

The laws of the land

The laws of the land govern one and all, or do they?

Is there one law for the rich and one for the poor?

One law for powerful nations and one for the weak?

One for Wall Street and one for Main Street?

Freedom is freedom as defined in law

True freedom is when the spirit runs free

Man can pass rules, edicts and resolutions

But my soul is free and no law can touch it

Giving up the state of nature for law, society and citizenship

But wherever you look man is bound by chains

Gurdjieff's man is in a state of slumber, walking along in indentured slavery

Steel coffins in the sky, a futuristic dystopia

Humankind trudges mechanically onwards seemingly blind and content

Consumed in the realm of Maya

The same vicious inexorable mythical metanarrative cruising the highways of time victoriously

But no one can legislate for my inner soul

The Little Master

Entering the world arena at seventeen
A tender shoot that remains evergreen

Watching in awe when you stand at the crease
And hit balls out of the park effortlessly without cease

Inspiration for a new generation
The little master, Cricket's batting sensation

The Lord Knows

The Lord knows all things

He knows what you've done, what you've said and what you've thought

The Lord knows all things

He knows your closely guarded secrets, your inner desires and wants

The Lord knows all things

He knows your failures, shortcomings and misdemeanours

The Lord knows all things

He knows what you would like to do, what will make you happy and what will leave you fulfilled

The Lord knows all things

He knows who will depart the Earth tonight and when you will depart the Earth

The Lord Knows.

The Lord's Hour

Darkness falls across the land

A cold chill runs down the spine

In the bleak mid-winter

The bitter frost bites and the blustery wind rages

In a world full of darkness a light will shine

That will brighten and illuminate one and all

A time of awakening and rebirth awaits

The Christmas hour is almost at hand

Hark! Exalt! Proclaim the Lord and King

He is born today in Bethlehem

The forsaken and downtrodden need not fear

The Lamb of God is here at last

Sing praises and rejoice

Glad tidings to everyone He will bring

Let not toils, snares and anger tear you down

Take heart in the Lord who always walks by your side

Although the path of life must be walked alone

The Lord will never forsake you

In times of joy and in the valley of despair

He will be there to offer comfort and support

Walk tall and spread the love of the Lord

Carry always a friendly smile and welcome all with an open heart

Fear not, fellow citizens of heaven and Earth

Your Lord is born in Bethlehem, Rejoice!

The lotus

Body, soul and mind

Stretching and straining

Into pure consciousness

Adept at the lotus posture

Breathing flows from chakra to chakra

Until the third eye glows

Equanimity of mind

Manifestations of immortal bliss

Spurts of joys as the soul ascends

Lost in the realm of yoga nidra

As the journey meanders from samsara to nirvana

Until the soul rises from the nadir of bandha to the apogee of
moksha

The man next door

Who is the man next door? I do not know

Shadows in the darkness and whispers through the walls

Grey smoke billows from an 18th century chimney

He emerges only when the full Moon beckons him

Gone is the manicured grass lawn and white picket fence

Instead a metaphorical fortress with CCTV, moat and trip wires

Besieged in the land of Pygmalion, a victim of the city's outward expansion

The man next door could one day turn out to be you

The man who believed in fairies

There once was a man who believed in fairies

Who walked in dark alleys in decaying cities

He believed he could fly and that he'd never die

And that everything would work out according to his to plan

One day on the Tube he called out to Delilah

The white fairy with golden hair who sang instead of speaking

Other passengers thought he was mad but he just felt glad

That he had a fairy that listened to him whenever he called

The morning rush hour

I always give myself enough time to get to work in the morning

Setting two alarms to ensure I don't craftily doze off after the
first one goes off

Initially I'm a bleary eyed automaton

Locked in the same daily robotic morning routine

Until 10.30 am when I come wide awake

After a cup of tea and a platter of chocolates

It's 7.30 am

Time to hit the street

The steady stream of commuters are flowing past

Like ants heeding the call to prayer

The usual pleasantries exchanged at the bus stop

No time to chat or I'll be late

Waiting as the first bus drives past without stopping

Already filled to capacity by fellow commuters

Now the bus stop gets packed and the jostling begins

As the next bus arrives the swords are out

Elbows flying, everyone trying to get that space

Standing room only, it's tight and it's hot

The perspiration of others, their coughs and their sneezes

A mobile phone rings, some still half asleep

Others in a dream, in their morning paper or listening to their mp3 player

Finally on the Tube, it's the end of the line

Hence I'm always guaranteed a seat

So I finally take my pick

Most days I read the broadsheets or a good book

But today I need some kip

So I shuffle a little and then relax in my seat

Like a dog on his basket settling himself before he takes a nap

Every few minutes the announcer keeps me informed where the train is

Luckily no delays, no jumpers, no signal failures or mechanical problems

I jump out at my destination a little refreshed

Eager to breathe fresh air once again

I stand on the right as I ascend the escalator

Unless I'm in a rush then I walk up on the left

I swipe my Oyster Card as I pass through the ticket barrier

And smile as the warm morning Sun hits my face

Then I'm bombarded with car horns and traffic jams

Confronted by frenzied delivery men and rushing city workers

The hustle and bustle of the city

An enchanting melody and surrealist cacophony of post modern living

Or a dystopia for those with extreme synaesthesia

I feel adrenaline, testosterone and a sense of combativeness in the air

At last I arrive at my office

My second home

I settle down at my desk

Take a few moments to ponder my trip

And the cute chick that smiled at me for a bit

I wonder what might have been if we'd both taken the time to chat for a bit

Suddenly the telephone rings and my colleagues shout "Hi"

I snap back into work

The morning commute now forgotten

Just another memory for the repository at the back of my mind

Until I commute again tomorrow morning

And there'll be another story to tell

The paralysis of analysis

Analyse, assess and articulate
Build, brainstorm and believe
Consider, contemplate and concur
Deliberate, debate and devour
Evaluate, examine and explore

When the mind is flooded with choices
The paralysis of analysis begins
Ask one hundred people to kindly opine
And one hundred different responses will be given

Unless the decision requires configuring and intangible sine or
cosine
Make the decision and take the jump
Solemnly proceed with a stern will and purpose

Be bold, brazen and brave, that is the only surmise
Engage energetically and forge forward

Don't wait for Christmas or the next leap year

The past

The haunted ghoul of one's own past
Slowly moulds into a leaden cast
A yellow brick road between the past and future
An individual journey with twists and turns

Life's journey involves a past and a future
But what if we live in the present and release all ego
Forget the constant struggle for status and conquest
And step off the ladder of accumulation and take in a deep
breath of fresh sea air

To live well we need so very little
But we're programmed to believe we need so very much
Let the synapses sparkle and smoulder with passion
As new ways of thinking liberate the soul

Awaken the spirit that lies within
Set your inner self free to breathe and explore

The perfumed garden

From the ancient rites of the Hiero Gamos and the Karma Sutra

To the lovers guide and the multiorgasmic tantric new age manuals

With virtual reality liaisons promising virtually real experiences

The 22st Century's perfumed garden will be a virtual tome

The same tree

We are all precious

We all breathe the same air

We all live under the same sky

We all live under the same Sun

We are all leaves from the same tree

We may be tall or short, large or small, black or white

We may be skilled in one thing and bad at another

We may be called to different vocations

We may be witty or dull, extrovert or introvert, happy or sad

We may be different leaves on different branches separated by a few centimetres or by a thousand miles

But we are all from the same tree.

The seasons

Spring breaks winters grasp and unlocks the tender light

The garden springs into life as the winter chill recedes

Tis time of Cerulean skies and fresh breezes from across the seas

Spring doth bring renewal, regeneration, new dreams and new vigour

Summer then effortlessly and majestically glides on through

Long warm days of barbeques and seaside escapades

Tis time of holidays, living in the great outdoors and relaxing in the shade

Summer doth bring energy, activity and unbounded bliss

Autumn draws in and the days slowly shorten

The leaves turn golden and the sunset crimson

Tis time of raucous soirees and iridescent skies

Autumn doth bring summer's retreat, nature's twilight and its transformation

Winter arrives like an unwelcome stranger in the night

Cold rainy days with grey skies and street lights being switched on at 3 pm

Tis time of office parties, tv dinners and six inch blankets of snow on the roads

Winter doth bring hibernation, introspection and transport stultification

The Secret Garden

It's quiet and calm by the old oak tree
The wooden cross a reminder
Time to reflect
Time to think

A sense of peace
A sense of tranquillity
The immense power of this spiritual place
The gateway to the universe

In the distance the Coral Sea
In the foreground swans glide majestically across the lake
A place of total serenity
Time stands still and hearts open wide

A place for believers and those still searching
A garden of daydreams
Of days dreaming of possibilities
And nights dreaming of fulfilment

Come rain, sun or winter snow
The garden welcomes everyone
Replete with secrets and fascinating tales
The secrets one day being revealed on cue to the few

Thesis

Married to my PhD thesis

That turned my life into a crisis

In the end I hoped to reach a state of catharsis

Instead I ended up in the cradle of psychosis

My prognosis dependant on my commitment to self-hypnosis

And all this over my PhD these

The soldiers

HM forces serving and defending the realm

Doing a valiant job in challenging circumstances

The dutiful rifleman, the vigilant brigadier, all possessing customary phlegm

All living life in harms way, all part of the foray

It is never easy to see what a soldier sees and feel what they feel

When comrades are hit and fall by their side

Technological advances can make war seem surreal

But the human face and the human price is very hard to hide

Whether in an Arctic pickle, an urban melee or a desert stew

There's an important job to do

Both home and abroad, and wherever they are called

Sometimes receiving too little acclaim for the brave job that they do

As Gordon Bassett witnesses the constant trail

The retinue of mourners as the entourages pass

They lived for the cause, so our liberty will prevail

The bugle rings out before the final mass but the sun will never set on any regiment

The Symbol

The red signet vibrates to the sound of music

Causing the translucent jellyfish in the aquarium to stir and
deposit red gold

Red gold is payment for the knowledge

The map showing the way to the deepest secret

The resting abode of the symbol

To be found hidden in the ether

Stretching from alpha to omega

Beyond the collective unconscious

The Tiger and the Cheetah

Once upon a time there was a great Tiger
King of the golfing world and respected by the masses

Brought down to his knees he has now emerged as a new Tiger
But can a Tiger really change his stripes and fulfil all his fans wishes?

From legendary superstar to serial adulterer
The descent has been swift

Giving in to the Id
The Shadow has taken control

Lurking in the background
Will always be his feline cousin the Cheetah

Always filling his path with temptations and enticing snares
Always waiting for another momentary weakness and the chance to pounce and capture the Self

His greatest battle will not be on the golf course
But in the cerebrum upstairs

He'll fight battles with the laws of karma
And struggle with the lure of the passions

His greatest glory will not be never falling

But in getting up, overcoming and learning from his transgressions

The treadmill

As a child
I was a little wild
I was like a curious squirrel
Who knew nothing of the treadmill's peril

In my teens
I was ever so lean
Floating free like a wild sea urchin
Rejecting the treadmill in favour of a pint at the Field and Firkin

In my youth
I was still searching for the truth
A workaholic shopaholic
Jumping on and off the treadmill in an inebriated frolic

In middle age
I felt like a sage
A zillion things to do and not enough time to do them
I was left succumbing to the treadmill but still clinging on to my
dreams

In old age
I was in the invalid's cage
Yet I was still drawn by the light

And the wish to demolish the treadmill so humanity could reach new heights

The tunnel

The tunnel is more than a funnel
For trains and cars to cross the English Channel

It's when you are in the zone
Always hitting the right tone

When everything seems like a dream
Like you are swimming in the cosmic stream

It's like the hand of god touched you on the shoulder
And gave you the power to move gigantic boulders

The ultimate truth?

Through myriad uncertainties and countless designs

I walk the eightfold path looking for aphorisms, maxims and epigrams

When the years roll by and time is recognisably finite

A new truth profoundly emerges, for there will be no more day after day and hour after hour

In the most unusual place and in the least expected encounter

The ultimate truth I may yet discover!

The Vibe Is King

I am the king and you are the queen
The Milky Way kid pumped full of caffeine

Lost in the jungles of Brunei or holding you tightly by the hand
The vibe is the addictive and contagious chemically laden magic wand

Birds sing salutations when spring arrives in the barren wastelands
And Gallipoli remembers the brotherhood tryst with the land

Far away traversing the Straits of Gibraltar
You know you will never falter

Hearts pound louder and louder before bursting into song
Pulsing inside you more powerfully than a ten tonne atom bomb

Lying down on deck chairs in warm and sunny Mediterranean pastures reminiscing, allegorizing or prophesising
Acknowledging that in the end the vibe is king

The Wire

A glimpse into the hidden world
Of Baltimore's most secret team
Listening in to all that talk
Punctuated by radio static and superfluous obscenities

With Mayor Royce and Carcetti
Police work is never free from political influence
Sometimes it is hard to make out head from tail
And stay above the water line

All I want is to get that wire
Do my job, that's the call of the hour
Avoid the judge's consternations and all the mire
And then relax in front of a log fire

The wrong side of the Thames

Could it be, that it was never meant to be

Because I was born on the wrong side of the Thames

She's too noble, too Grenoble, too much scones, golf and croquet

I'm too much of a fable, like designer labels, too much burgers,
mountain bikes and football

At first it was hot, the passion most wild

We both thought we were destined to be

As time ticked on we became many shades of grey

Instead of the fiery red, dazzling yellow and outdoorsy green

Or maybe it was, whether we liked it or not

We came from different sides of the Thames

No matter the chatter, we marched forward together

We fought for our love

Because it was sent from above

On the winds of a dove

We vanquished all obstacles

Including the fact that we came from opposite sides of the
Thames

They know not

They know not what they do
For they are all too human
Filled with insatiable desires from the primal fire
Fragmented from the whole and living in a hole

They may think they are superhuman
But Zarathustra will disagree
Living life as detached pieces of a jigsaw
Ignorant of the beauty of the cosmic tapestry

Think of Jason

From the mothers womb a second time
A second coming and a second chance to shine

Archimedes and Osho chatting in the backseat
Boris Johnson and George Osborne firmly in the driving seat

A new chapter can always be written
If faith and hope are never forgotten

Through the prism of the prison

Aperture 1

No more Sun kissed days lazing on Clapham Common

No more football matches and no more swimming in the sea

No more running carefree on Epsom Downs and Richmond Park, just like in times of yore

No more women, drink, drugs, gigs and raves

If you can't do the time then don't do the crime

Or so they say, but all I know is that they want me to pay

A cacophony of lies my speciality, love playing with fire, but so do we all

Thrill of the kill, the fast and the furious, always unstoppable even behind bars

Aperture 2

These four walls closing in

Can't stand it no more, I need oxygen

The anger builds up, the incessant ticking of the clock

Hour after hour, day after day, my life drifting away

Luckily it wasn't Clink or the pain and soul corrosion

Raw skin on blunt rusted metal and coagulating blood on decaying damp floors

The usual landscape, the forsaken and the forgotten

Misaligned, misunderstood, misconstrued and misjudged

Aperture 3

The screws know the score, this is HMP

This is their job, their way to earn their bread

But this is my life, a bird in a cage, another lamb to the slaughter

Incarceration, institutionalisation, indignation, that's life inside

Recalcitrant's and recidivists come back here again

To be under the constant glare of the prison's watchful eye

Bentham's panopticon cannot be the solution to society's ills

Convict rehabilitation, slashing reoffending, tackling the causes of malfeasance and delinquency, is that so?

Thunderstorms in the Highlands

Being in the middle of a thunderstorm in the Scottish Highlands was exhilarating. In the distance the dark voluptuous rainclouds hug the mountain peaks and drift slowly towards you. A chill runs down the spine as the first drops of rain hit your skin and the sudden bursts of lightening light up the horizon. The atmosphere feels electric and suddenly everything stops. Nature in its unadulterated glory is speaking.

Then it starts to rain a type of rain that's warm and soothing. The soft droplets of rain engulf you and as the rainclouds above grow larger and larger you begin to feel as if they may plunge down and embrace you.

Next you hear the faint rumbling of thunder in the distance. The rumbling gets closer and closer and you know it's going to be a big and powerful thunderstorm. As the storm approaches goose bumps appear all over your skin and you tingle all over in anticipation.

When the storm reaches overhead you completely let go and let the power of nature engulf you. It's now when you feel so close to nature, totally at one with nature. You experience your senses being stimulated by nature's mighty power.

Your body sparkles and shudders as the storm completely overwhelms you, the momentum of the storm keeps going until finally when the storm passes you are left with a calm wonderful experience which you can reflect on for a long time.

You feel exhilarated to have experienced the raw intensity and wild unrestrained energy of nature.

Time

The sands of time don't stand still

Not for me and not for you

From the beginning to the end

The sands of time have seen what was and they will see what
will be

The sands of time keep flowing

Through the hour glass somewhere in the sky

As time marches on relentlessly

Each minute on Earth becomes more precious

The world is still a slave

To the shackles of the great equaliser

Not even the Prince of Persia can control

The heavenly sands of time

The sands of time will not wait

And neither will fate, so never hesitate

Or you'll be too late, to catch the bait that fell off the crate of
good fortune

And into your palm, like an ever blessed psalm

Time on type

In work, in sports, in aviation, in the war zone, in law, in
business and in politics

The more experience you have the greater the view

To see the woods from the trees

To fit together the last pieces of the jigsaw

To see through the vortex and solve the matrix

Time on type is what counts.

Together

I can see the moonlight in your eyes every time I go to sleep

I can see the sunlight in your eyes every time I awake

I can see the desire in your eyes as I kiss you ever so gently

I can see the longing and beckoning in your eyes when you hold me tight

I can read your thoughts by looking deep into your eyes

I can feel my heart race wildly as you look deeply into my eyes

I can smell your delicious scent as it lingers above your perfume when you lean in close to kiss me

I can feel your pulse and heartbeat as I hold you in my arms

Touring cars

A never-ending stream of faces and places
Too many to fathom

The plethora of sights and smells merge into one
A retinue of optic imprints

T-R-A-N-C-E

As you read these words you allow yourself to let your mind
wander

Just STOP and imagine yourself drifting away

To a place of joy and happy memories

Inside a bubble of warm fuzzy energy

As your breathing s-l-o-w-s d-o-w-n

You find yourself feeling c-a-l-m and r-e-l-a-x-e-d

Not a care in the world

OPEN YOURSELF to this wonderful experience

SURRENDER fully and LET IT HAPPEN

IMAGINE YOURSELF doing the things you always wanted

AS YOU BEGIN TO FEEL that warmth within

Tree of love

You are the tree planted by the Lord
Your roots going back generations

Your branches reach to heaven above
Each leaf a brand new day

Upon your branch there perched a dove
Enamoured by the tree of love

Tuition Fees

Protesting in the bitter cold live on TV
So the whole wide world can see
That many oppose the rise in tuition fees
Tuition fees don't fill students with glee

Politicians in a pickle pondering what to decree
Liberal Democrats wishing they could foresee
How broken election promises will leave their party in a calamity
Tuition fees don't fill students with glee

Kettled in and dying for a pee
Wishing they never had that extra coffee
Feeling weak in the knee and wishing they could flee
Tuition fees don't fill students with glee

Parents let their kids run free
Fear of building up crippling debt putting kids off studying for a degree
If only university education was again free!
Tuition fees don't fill students with glee

Twin turbo

Stuck in the grind
A tailback on the M25
Another tricky junction
A typical frenzied roundabout
Twin turbo to the rescue
Gets me out of trouble in a jiffy

Waiting at the traffic lights
Other cars start revving
Thinking it'll get me sweating
Not knowing I have old painless
Hidden under the bonnet

When the amber light comes on
And the engines begin pounding
Twin turbo will whisk me away
As I fly by while they drive by
As other cars lost in my tail smoke

Twitter

A twitter here and a twatter there
Bebo and I will Hi 5 you
Friends Reunited past and present
Orkut we make it full of E-Harmony

My twitter voyage began with a solitary one liner
I now have created a whole blog
The voyage has no final destination
But hath a life all to itself

I am like a servant forced to record my innermost thoughts
Sometimes I feel I delve too deep into thine very core
I feel naked because the whole world can see my soul laid bare
A voyeuristic fantasy that's now a reality

My live is revolving
Just as the Earth keeps turning
And my twitter live feed records it all
The drama, the highs and the lows

Let's all get connected
Get wired even more
Where will this end nobody knows
Perhaps I'll end up half machine and half homo sapien?

Mr. Aldous Huxley, all human, all prescient

How did you foresee all you did!?

I still don't know what fate has in store

A brave new world that we'll all have to explore

Ugly duckling

The ugly duckling from Brummie in need of love

Shunned by the masses but with a heart purer than a dove

Her personality captivates even a downtrodden suicidal drunk

But most men would prefer she was locked up in someone's trunk

For a few moments here and there she is treated with a modicum of decency

Her face lights up and she looks like a member of the regency

And at last she transforms into a swan and brims with joy

Her beauty glowing brighter than Helen of Troy

Until men again become shallow and send her to the gallows

Forcing the ugly duckling to eschew mankind and live life hidden in the meadows

She sings with spritely sparrows and enjoys looking up at serenading swallows

Yet her brow always remains furrowed because she only appears in the shadows

Umbrella

The umbrella

Is my most sturdiest fella

He may be telescopic, extendable or golf

But he is of no use sitting on the shelf

Many a time I have ventured out without my sturdy fella

I end up drenched

And my teeth tightly clenched

Kicking myself for forgetting my umbrella

Universal connection

If you look through the universe's spectacles

You will see the ants, snails, hares, foxes, and creatures you always overlook

You will see the plants, shrubs, flowers and grass you sometimes trample upon

All living creature in the universe are interconnected and integral to the whole

Just as every moment of every day you are interconnected and integral to the whole

Unofficial Legislator

Poetic licence to say what one may

A lyrical commentary on what some may feel hesitant to say

The soul of the poet always flies freely and without sway

This verse may not be enacted or enter the statute book

Yet the unofficial legislator always ensures an alternative outlook

His verse recording an imprint of life as it was when it was written

Forever to be saved in the Doomsday book

Unrequited love

Sometimes you feel you know the one you love
Only for the passing wind to blow them away
Sometimes you write your beloved's name across your heart
Only for the salty sea to wash it away

Unstoppable

In the forest of Brunei facing a 1000 foot cliff

The last mile of the London marathon and your legs are giving out

Climbing to the top of Everest in low visibility and the weather is getting worse

Unstoppable is the only way

You've been diagnosed with cancer and things are not looking good

You've had a heart attack and are always short of breath

The doctor has predicted you have only 180 days to live

Unstoppable is the only way

Your husband cheated on you and you feel like giving up

You've lost your job and your kids are playing up

Your best friend betrayed you and you don't feel like making up

Unstoppable is the only way

You were in a road accident, now you're paraplegic and you don't feel like getting up

You've been bullied, harassed, mistreated and you're always fired up

You think you're too short, too fat, too this or too that and don't think you can rise up

Unstoppable is the only way

Until I retire

The morning rush hour is ever so dire

Always caught in the mire

No time for a shower

A dose of caffeine to ensure I don't tire

Caught in the incessant rhythm of the diurnal gyre

Still counting the days until I retire

Until sunrise

Let me love you all night long
Let me relieve you of all those longings

Let me fulfil your secret fantasies
Let us walk in the perfumed garden

Let our bodies dance in rhythm
Let our bodies cast erotic candlelit shadows on the wall

Let me feel the warmth of your touch
Let me feel your sweet caress

Let me explore your body
Let me feel your hands all over

Let me feel your mouth all over
Let me feel your body all over

Let us melt into pure energy
Let us melt into raw passion

Let us melt into insatiable desire
Let us melt into each other

Let us drown in each others embrace

Let us drown in this night of ecstasy

Let us unite tonight
Let us love tonight

Until we meet again

The greatest mum so full of grace
Sent from above and guided by faith
The love she showed was beyond compare
The immense happiness she brought to one and all

An angel now resting in Elysium's palace
Looking down upon us with the warmest smile
Radiating benevolence and warmth on the coldest nights
Her compassion and care embraced everyone she met

Each day she brought new rays of light
Each day she gave of her very best
From Trinidad to London and wherever she went
She was a talisman of hope and beacon of joy

The most amazing free spirit that traversed the Earth
Spreading love and kindness to the meek and strong
She eschewed materialism and gave herself fully to selfless love
A child of God now united with the Almighty One

Through thick and thin, her faith steered her through
Though many dangers, toils and snares abounded
The darkest night and the harshest storm never made her doubt
A great mind, divine spirit and a heavenly soul

O greatest mum how great thou were

You'll be sorely missed beyond what words can convey

I will hold your dreams close to my heart

I will remember the words you held so dear

Urban foxes

Urban foxes scampering around in the night

Suburban carnivores colonising the gardens, sheds and outhouses

Surfing under cover of darkness and away from the street light

Ravaging through alleyways, scavenging in bins and burrowing under greenhouses

Playing and screeching with sheer delight

Battling with humans in a game of cat and mouse

Ducking and diving through the high street traffic

Stealthily and cunningly manoeuvring back to their secret lair

Scrounging and searching for the next tasty picnic

Earnestly trying to avoid being ensnared

Scrawly and scrawny, a part of the urban fabric

Uncannily possessed with a knack for survival, crafty street wise canines appearing out of nowhere

Uwin

Uwin some

You lose some

Until you reach the home of the lithesome cerebrum

Uwin is the place to go if you want to get smart

Developing academic prowess is only the start

Even love can be found if you open your heart

Valentine's Day

The cold February days, the dawn of spring, two songbirds sing a sweet melody

Every quattordici febbraio, the day of lovers, is a reminder that love is a harmonious symphony

Soul to soul, heart to heart and hand in hand, the songbirds glide along on an enchanted journey

At night in their dreams, as the universe sleeps, Cupid's golden arrow penetrates their hearts and melts into pure energy.

Magical feelings spread warmth from deep inside, emotions suddenly igniting and fulfilling the heart and soul

You go through life waiting for the one, that special connection that makes life incredible and complete.

Vibrant and enthralling is the songbirds dance, mesmerising and captivating like the rays of the Sun

As they soar so incredibly high in the clear blue sky, exploring the mountains, cities, oceans and beaches

Leaving all their troubles, concerns and worries behind

Experiencing the wonderful vistas that the world has to offer, together so happy and so carefree

Nature's most incredible and most powerful experience of falling in love

Time seems to stand still and each moment seems eternal

In sickness and in health, in the good times and the bad

Nothing can stop this beautiful rhapsody

Every beat of their hearts bringing the songbirds closer, until they're united as one and filled with pure ecstasy

Valentine Text

I was going to give you a million pounds and a luxury country
homestead

But I know you would prefer this text instead

Because two hearts beating as one

Is worth more than a ton

I will give you the sun, moon and stars

Just to see your beautiful smile from afar

Even though we are sometimes apart

You are always in my heart

Vespers

O God, come to my aid
O Lord, make haste to help me

The hymns, psalms and Magnificat
The crepuscular prayers as the darkness draw in

Reflection of a day just passed
Reflection of the night to come

A journey on the battlefield of life
A journey walked only by faith

I pray that all my questions are answered
I pray that all my doubts are allayed

The path ahead may be uncertain but my faith is rejuvenated
The path of life may take me far from safety but I face it with a welcoming smile and full of grace

As Compline begins and the day draws to a close
I go to sleep but not before I commend my spirit into the Lord's hands

If I die tonight I know the Lord has a place for me in heaven
If I die tonight I know I will be reborn with eternal life

Until the wings of dawn summon me from slumber

Until Lauds and a new day begins, until I give thanks and praise to the one who gives me the day and gave me my life

Virtual dreaming

Lying awake in the night
The stars and Moon shining so bright

Is this real or am I dreaming?
Images of bacchanalia leave me simmering

Vladimir

A time for heroes is at hand
When all the world shifts like sand

When values falter and retreat
The weak fall to their feet

Until an magnetic athletic leader emerges with an empowering vision
The lives of the nation, he will brighten!

Voice in the trenches

In the distance the sentry asked "who goes there?"

But no reply was heard

Only an eerie echo

That reverberated across the silent night

Between the interstices of the echo

Others voice were heard

Voices of despair

That were as biting as the night's unbearable frost

As the spectre of brinkmanship grew over the world

The trenches of the Somme grew darker as each minute passed

The sentry's spirit whispered

"Will there be a star in heaven for each of the fallen?"

Volcanic fury

Far beneath the Earth's crust
The sorceress wields her fiery spell
Thunder and brimstone and molten rock
The cauldron simmers past boiling point

Spewing scorching volcanic ash into the freezing midnight sky
The cataclysmic volcanic fury lighting up the periphery
When nature lets loose, it's magnificent to see
A message to mankind, nature will have the last laugh

Shutting down air traffic along the length and breadth of
Western Europe
Airports deserted and passengers stranded across the globe
When nature lets loose, it's magnificent to see
A message to mankind, nature will have the last laugh

Voulez-vous coucher avec moi ce soir

Spend the night with me
Love me like there is no tomorrow

Continue undressing me with your eyes
Until our clothes lie in a mangled heap on the bedroom floor

Step into the waterfall, feel the surge of the waves
Let the beads of sweat cascade down your naked body

I feel the rush, the adrenaline and the emotion
I feel the fire burning inside your body

Your moans and screams drive me wild
Let us erupt like Vesuvius and let our lava overflow freely

Waiting

Waiting for the evening to have that great meal

Waiting for the weekend to hit that great club

Waiting for next month to party at your friends wedding

Waiting for the summer to go on holiday and hit the sun drenched beaches

Waiting until you passed your test so you can hit the road with your new car

Waiting until you've got that great job so you can splash out and live large

Waiting until you meet the right partner so you can have the relationship you've always dreamed of

Waiting until you've got that great apartment so you can live the life you've always wanted to

Why are we waiting? Life is what happens when you are making other plans.

Walking in the desert

Walking in the desert for forty days and forty nights

Searching for the refuge of Mount Sinai

The storm beats down and rattles every bone

And all hope seems lost as the desert wind rises and wails

The skin becomes blistered by the searing daytime desert heat

And the body freezes from the ice cold desert night

But when all hope seemed lost a star in the sky shone and twinkled

God, the creator of one and all, is watching

Walking on china

Cuts beneath the feet

Blisters from walking barefoot along the street

Eggs shells line the path

Where the politically correct fear to tread

King Henry summons the censor

The Long Parliament passes the law

Oliver Cromwell's campaign fuels the diaspora

A fatwa to haunt the net savvy fashionistas

What if life was a holiday?

What if life was a holiday?

Party all day and party all night

Live it up, live it large and live it fast

From the moment the plane lands it is time for a blast

Drinking copious amounts of Mojitos, Mai Tais and Tequila Sunrises

Dancing insouciantly under the bright discothèque lights until the sun rises

Addicted to the sandy beach and the azure blue sea

And an endless procession of scantily clad twentysomethings living carefree

When you're away

When you're away my love for you grows stronger
Sweet like strawberry ice cream my heart does hunger

Your warm hugs keep me warm like the rays of the morning sun
Two lovebirds singing and dancing and having lots of fun

We dance and sing on the beach and watch the golden sunset
Listening to sweet songs and singing romantic duets

Every night in my dreams I see us laughing and smiling
Walking hand in hand and falling asleep cuddling

A moment of bliss
I miss your gentle kiss

The wind carries this poem across the land, sea and air
Until it whispers each word softly and gently in your ear

We may sometimes be apart
But you are always in my heart

In the good times and the bad, whether it is hot or cold,
You're my sweet baby in the whole world

Who I Am

There is the image that I think I am
But that is not who I am

There is what my friends, family and colleagues think I am
But that is not who I am

There is my physical being, my curious character and my
gregarious personality
But that is only a mirror of who I am

I am fluid, ever changing
Growing and decaying
Born afresh and dying daily

I am the soul beyond the physical mirror

Who will I reach today?

As lunchtime approaches, I ponder
What good deeds have I done so far today?
How many lives have I touched or changed for the better?

Any changes may be subtle, imperceptible and forgotten later
All it takes is a smile, a good word
Or a little time and a listening ear

Still the day is young and in my travels I can reach out
And make the world a little happier as I go on my walkabout
Everyday is a day of giving and of celebration

Windowsill

Looking out at the world so bright

Looking out at the mesmerizing stars at night

From the window of my world I can see

From the window of your world you also see

We sit safe inside our rooms with a view looking on with equanimity

We sit observing life's unfolding tapestry

Winter Solstice 2012

Some say the end of the world is nigh

That in 2012 the final curtain will fall

When the planets will collide and the world will end

The Mayans prediction of the great doomsday

Leaves historians in a pickle and novelists in a stew

Arguing over who said what, when and what it all means

Any new theory will eventually have counter theories

And any theory can metamorphosise from revisions and reengineering

Even if it passes Popper's falsifiability

The new age of Aquarius is set to begin as the old age of Pisces retreats

Every few years a new hypothesis captures the public's imagination

A predilection for novelty, mysticism, shamanism and eschatology; enough to create a viral cyber frenzy

Will 2012 bring Armageddon and will the four horsemen of the apocalypse roam the Earth?

Or will we end up studying Noetic science and developing our sixth sense?

Which revelations will be proved true? We shall have to wait and see!

Worth

Stop and step into a place of awakening

Where your heart opens to holy yearning

Silence grips each pore and leaves you pondering

And you connect to a new spiritual dimension and begin exploring

The further you look inside yourself the closer you come to the centre of the universe

Inspired by God's word and each poignant verse

Once the road you knew has disappeared and there are no sign posts to guide you

You walk by faith as God leads and protects you from harm and voodoo

Walk in the Quiet Garden and among the reeds you will find satisfaction

A simple menu of Lectio divina, prayer and quiet reflection

Let Worth be the sanctuary where your spirit grows beyond compare

Finding happiness, peace and fulfilment is closer than you had previously been aware

Yasmine

Each night I observe the outline of your face

Your pretty green eyes
Your curly blonde hair
Your satin lingerie

Lost in your arms
Lost in your embrace

My body hungers for you
My heart yearns for you

You soothe me with your touch
You nourish me with your kiss
You intoxicate me with your body

Your love keeps me alive

Yoga

Yogic breathing and yogic chanting
Auditory pleasure and a cerebral tonic

Yogic stretching and yogic postures
Physical rejuvenation and toxin cleansing

Practicing surya namaskara once per day
Keeps the doctor away

Yogic Chant

o

om

om m

om ma

om man

om mani

om mani p

om mani pa

om mani pad

om mani padm

om mani padme

om mani padme h

om mani padme hu

om mani padme hum

om mani padme hum

om mani padme hum

om mani padme hum

om mani padme hum

om mani padme hum

om mani padme hu

om mani padme h

om mani padme

om mani padm

om mani pad

om mani pa

om mani p

om mani

om man

om ma

om m

om

o

[repeat as required]

Zeynep

Every night when I fall asleep I dream a dream

Of us together on the beach laughing and sipping Bailey's Irish Cream

Dancing together in the iridescent moonlight

Until the first rays of early morning sunlight

Whenever you look into my eyes

My temperature starts to rise

My heart skips a beat

Each time you hug me when we greet

Only you can take me higher

And fuel the flames of desire

We may sometimes be apart

But you are always in my heart

20/20 life

Thousands of fans cheer and others drink beer
The stands are alight with crowds clad in fluorescent colours

Sitting in the pavilions in the serenity of their seat
They share glimpses of history and glimpses of greatness

Only the brave will step up to the plate
A slip here, a fine line there, an edge behind and they'll celebrate

One six, one lbw, one decision the batsman's way
He faced inescapable defeat but now victory smiles his way

One over left and the batsman can be the king
His name will ring out as the crowd erupts in song

He play from the heart living only to win
He'd rather die at the crease than let his spirit give in

Each minute, each second, each sinew he must strain
He lives in the moment, he can't feel any pain

Each bodily cell sparks brightly when he's called on to play
He'll make it a day of days and all will go his way

Time slows down and he visualises everything in slow motion

Each ball, each bounce and the bowler's arm flexion

He's focused solely on good line and length

His body's instant metamorphosis, now he possesses
superhuman strength

From tasting loss and the unyielding unforgiving iron clasp of
defeat

It's a bitter sweet triumph and now he's ecstatically upbeat

The wild adrenaline pumping joy of 20/20 sets pulses racing

Long live 20/20 and its spectacular extravagant jousting

360°

I am a fly

my eyes!

watching

you with all